THE SHADOWED BED

Jack Clemo

Jack Clemo was born in a small Cornish clayworkers' cottage in 1916. By his nineteenth birthday Jack had become too deaf to hear conversation, and his condition steadily worsened. By this time, though, he had determined to become a writer. His first novel *Wilding Graft* was published in 1948 and won the Atlantic Award in Literature from Birmingham University. A. L. Rowse (the Cornish writer and critic) wrote: 'He is of the spiritual progeny of that greatest of West Country writers, Thomas Hardy.'

Clemo's first autobiography, *Confession of a Rebel*, was published in 1949. In it Clemo described his life up to the age of thirty with great intensity, and showed how his Christian faith — rejected as superstition by many of his contemporaries — had enabled him to find his place in the world, despite his handicaps. The book, like many of Clemo's, divided his critics.

By 1955 Jack Clemo had gone completely blind. In 1958 his book *The Invading Gospel* was published, which was a personal statement of his faith which had given him hope as blindness approached. In 1961 he was awarded a Civil List pension for his service to English literature. In the same year, a collection of his earlier poetry was published, *The Map of Clay*. This was followed by *Cactus on Carmel* (1967), *The Echoing Tip* (1971), *Broad Autumn* (1975) and *A Different Drummer* (1986). His volume of humorous stories and verse, *The Bouncing Hills*, was published in 1983.

The extraordinary story of his marriage in 1968 to Ruth Peaty was described in his second autobiography *Marriage of a Rebel*, published in 1980. This story is also told in Sally Magnusson's book, *Clemo: A Love Story*.

In 1970 Jack Clemo was crowned *Prydyth an Pry* (Poet of the Clay) at the Cornish Gorsedd festival. He also received an honorary D.Litt. from Exeter University in 1981. His early life was the subject of a BBC drama documentary, *A Different Drummer*, in 1980.

The Shadowed Bed was first drafted in 1938, and was rewritten in the late 1940s and revised again in 1985. Its final revision was made after Jack Clemo had moved from Cornwall to Dorset. It is published here nearly fifty years after Clemo first started it.

The Shadowed Bed

A Novel

Jack Clemo

Tring · Batavia · Sydney

Copyright © 1986 Jack Clemo

Published by
Lion Publishing plc
Icknield Way, Tring, Herts, England
ISBN 0 7459 1122 6
Albatross Books Pty Ltd
PO Box 320, Sutherland, NSW 2232, Australia
ISBN 0 86760 833 1

First edition 1986

Printed and bound in Great Britain by
Cox and Wyman, Reading

Contents

PART ONE   THE BARRICADE   9
PART TWO   THE INVASION   71
PART THREE   THE SLAIN   157

You snatched the opposing shovel
Near the orchard, under the pit-waste cone:
My life soon followed and had to be sane.
Clay-dust on the cancelled apple
Bade me close your foreign mine.

Sunken now is the farm's lap
Where my journey was jolted;
The shadowing headstocks have decayed.
But you hand me tools on a green lip
Somehow cleansed for my art and creed.

Preface

This novel embodies the primitive 'clay-bed' mysticism which inspired my early poems. Most of the tale was written during the same period as the poetry, and while I lived in the gritty region of Cornwall which I describe.

Anne Treneer once stated that the clay fantasy on the uplands behind St Austell is 'like an allegory by C. S. Lewis.' I may have had something of Lewis's motive in shaping my village drama, in which an almost medieval imagination haunts a weird patch of modern industry. The surface narrative depicts the clay country as it was about 1950, when remote hamlets were still only partly modernized and the natives were often a raw and strident breed. Some of the characters are portraits of people I knew in my youth who are now dead. Carn Veor itself, however, is an invented village and not, like the Meledor of my earlier novel, *Wilding Graft*, an actual place which the reader could visit. The pagan hypnotism exerted by Beale through Rosa and Florrie is, of course, entirely fictitious and belongs more to the allegorical side of the tale, but those who dislike allegory can read the book as the record of a strange conflict between darkly occult and benevolently magnetic forces.

J. C.

Part One

The Barricade

Heap me over
From this tremendous Lover:
Float thy vague veil about me, lest He see!

Francis Thompson

Chapter One

ALL through the morning the dam had risen, crisp and glacial in the March sunshine. An excavator had crunched to and fro along the base of the clay-dump, scooping out a broad ditch and piling the refuse in a solid barrier above it. Workmen with shovels had ridged the bank and fastened sheets of corrugated iron against the inner wall. The dump was an old one, abandoned years ago and now deeply fissured, but yesterday's rainstorm had broken the peak, two hundred feet up; several tons of sand had been swept down through the gullies and poured over the low hedge into the village lane. Some of it had fanned out into the gutter farthest from the dump, but cone-shaped mounds still remained on the nearer side awaiting the arrival of lorries to remove them. Fifty yards off a rope was slung between a telegraph pole and a field gatepost, barring the road to traffic.

Joe Gool, who was working on the dam early in the afternoon, was not a paid labourer. He had come to the site when these men left it, and yielded to a whim, seeking some exertion before he met Bronwen Cundy. He was a tall gaunt fellow in his late twenties, obviously a native. The stark grey background suited him; he looked upon the general mess with stolid enjoyment as he added boulders, whitened gorse twigs and frayed clotted hazel boughs to the structure. His pale face had something of the wrenched, warped perversity of the landscape; he seemed to commune with the coldly volcanic clay-world, knowing its vagaries and loving them.

11

At length he straightened and stood with a hand on the raised scoop of the excavator. His black eyes narrowed upon the clear stretch of the lane winding southward into agricultural country, but they had lost the glow of expectancy that set him working. Bronwen had now appeared around the bend, moving under clouds of white steam that puffed out at intervals from an engine-house adjoining the sand-dump. She was not alone, however: beside her walked a slight, black-garbed figure, a middle-aged clergyman — the Rev. Felix Reed, who had been installed as vicar of this remote village of Carn Veor only last Sunday. Joe felt resentful that Bronwen should have met the vicar on her homeward journey, and that his own meeting with her was to be spoilt, stiffened into formality by the presence of a chilling stranger.

Slowly he scrambled down from the barricade into the gravel ditch and lurched past the excavator, along behind the sandbanks until he came to a gap in the hedge. Refuse had gathered here also in soft wet drifts, and after climbing over the dam he was forced to keep close to the granite wall as he passed through into the roadway. He halted in the centre of the lane, shifted his cap aggressively and waited the couple's approach.

They ducked under the rope, Mr Reed a little stiffly, holding the brim of his hat to prevent it from being knocked off, his spectacles flashing out into sunlight from the shadow of his arm. Bronwen waved gaily at Joe as she bobbed up on the nearer side. When they reached the edge of the spilled sand they walked in single file, Bronwen leading the way, following the tortuous ruts that rain had bored through the refuse. Bronwen moved in little jumps and side-steps, caring no more than Joe to appear elegant in the vicar's presence. She was taller than the clergyman, her thick gingery hair fluffed out

12

under a green beret. Her face, like Joe's, was large-boned, with a heavy stubborn chin, but her complexion was swarthy, heightening to red beneath the small grey eyes, which darted about with a sort of blithe vexation. Her mouth was very wide and full-lipped, naturally a sensual mouth, but not yet coarsened by awareness of adult, stale womanhood. There was no feminine daintiness or delicacy either in her face or her manners; her appeal was rather that of rude female strength, well suggested by the big brown hands with their long, hard powerful fingers. She was still only seventeen, an undiluted Cornish type of village girl, obviously masterful and possessive, capable of impulsive tenderness but not softly yielding, not soft even in the flesh, but moulded in a firm, raw texture of vitality.

As she drew near Joe noted from the pouting of her lips that she was not to be entirely cheated because Mr Reed was with her. Joe felt equally resolved, and when at last she halted in front of him they gripped hands and kissed, loosely and clumsily on the mouth.

'You're very tidy — as usual!' she greeted, laughing down at her hand as she withdrew it, muddied from Joe's clasp. 'What've you been doing?'

'Getting ready for work.' Joe's voice sounded strained in its humour; he glanced warily back at Mr Reed.

The vicar had paused discreetly several yards away and was peering across at some goats that were grazing tethered to the boughs of hazel clumps, on a broad turfed beacon that rose just outside the village, to the southwest. His face looked blotchy in the sunlight — a round, plump face, but with a coldness and acidity about it, the marks of a mind which, in both its affirmations and denials, was following a fashion, having no personal revelation to steady or convince it.

13

He heard the pair draw apart and came forward awkwardly, addressing Joe with reserve:

'Good afternoon, Mr Gool!'

'Good afternoon, sir!' replied Joe, again freshened and uninhibited. 'I daresay Bron's told you all about me coming along the road?'

'A little,' said the vicar, smiling faintly.

'We've made plenty o' talk here lately,' Joe went on. 'Only started to court openly a few months ago. Up to then 'twas a indoor affair, and that looks a bit fishy — natural it should, I s'pose.'

'Probably so, in a village. Of course your health . . .'

'Yes, I've got to make up for lost time. I was cooped in most of the winters through my teens — often in bed for weeks . . . But that's no excuse for getting sly with a neighbour's maid under your own roof — or so folks is saying. I don't reckon we're much in your line, any more'n the scenery is.'

The vicar shrugged with distaste, jerking his hand towards the sprawled gritty crust of mud that surrounded them.

'These roads!' he muttered. 'Why doesn't Mr Beale fence them off more efficiently from the refuse heaps?'

Joe laughed, meeting the vicar's eye with a perverse glint of mockery.

'You're like the rest of us, sir — beginning to ask questions about Beale. We spend most of our time in Carn Veor doing that — except when we're asking questions about Potter. And we're left guessing both ways. We've just got to put up with things as they are.'

Bronwen had slipped her arm through his, and the trio moved slowly forward, walking now abreast, Bronwen between the two men. Mr Reed still kept to the rain-cleared channels, but the girl trod cautiously, often on tiptoe, upon the thin hardening edges of sand;

14

while Joe, who wore heavy boots and clay-smeared corduroy trousers, pushed stolidly through whatever lay in his path.

'No pretty place to live in, sir, if you got refined tastes of any sort,' he resumed, the aggressive banter showing that he was still nettled at the lack of privacy between him and Bronwen, the inability to release himself in normal contacts, which made her pressure on his arm almost irritating. 'We've got to rough it here and get used to the queernesses. When we aren't washed out with sand we're nearly choked out with smoke — and not just ordinary smoke from the claywork stacks. 'Tis the smoke of buildings going up in flames.'

Mr Reed looked puzzled, apprehensive.

'You mean — accidents, I suppose?'

'No, sir — unless people can be mesmerized by accident. It's got something to do with a very mystifying girl here — Rosa Nance.'

'I've heard of the girl,' replied Mr Reed, frowning slightly and lowering his eyes as he followed a curve of the rut towards the barricade. 'In fact, I saw her a few nights ago with — er — Mr Truscott, the boxer.'

'Oh yes — Bert,' responded Joe. 'He was always her favourite, but his will-power's as hard as his fists — he just takes what he wants and can't be drawn in any further. It's different with some o' the other fellows who work around Beale's pits. Rosa puts her spell on 'em, but it goes twisted — something else comes through and they set fire to the place where they've been with her.'

'Are these outbreaks frequent?' enquired the vicar.

'Common enough, sir. It caught on like a mania once it started. Every month or two there's a flare in the sky — some tip-cuddy or tool-shed ablaze: Beale even lost a big dry-kiln last August over at Henstone where Bron's father works. We don't think Rosa herself wants the

15

fellows to use a match-box under the sacking or news-
papers or some old coat hanging on a nail — and we
don't think it's just guilty conscience. The men seem
mesmerized, as I said, like chaps acting funny under
dope — though of course their wives or aunts won't take
that as an excuse.'

Bronwen received this witticism with an uneasy
laugh, but Mr Reed's manner hardened to severity.

'And doesn't Beale inform the police of this disgraceful behaviour?'

'No, he don't interfere at all. He's a magistrate and
could stop it if he wanted to. But he don't even pull the
men into court when they burn down his buildings.
He's a queer fellow, and 'tis a queer place you've come
to. Things go on here that'd never be allowed in any
straightforward piece o' Cornwall . . . Have you seen
Beale yet, Mr Reed?'

'Only in his car as he drives back to the manor from
his office here. But I — er — have an appointment with
him this afternoon.' The vicar spoke superciliously, as if
wishing to emphasize that he had now begun moving
among his social equals, the local gentry, and must be
treated with respect.

Joe did not become more polite, however; he whistled.

'When! That's quick work. But I'd expect it o' Beale.
He's no church-goer but he always likes to get thick with
the parsons here. He was hand-in-glove with Ashford as
long as I knew him. Very different from Potter, who
gives our parsons the go-by as a rule. You haven't seen
him yet, I'll warrant.'

'No, I've not yet been approached by Mr Potter. I
understand that he and Beale are — well, not on the
best of terms.'

'That's putting it mild,' commented Joe, somewhat
more grimly than he had spoken hitherto. 'The fight

16

they're staging has been the talk o' Carn Veor ever since I can remember, though they don't neither of 'em live in the village.'

Joe glanced at Bronwen as she pushed her arm further through his until their fingers knotted in together. He felt the pressure of her hand, a nervous, even fearful clutch, as if the subject they were discussing, as well as the vicar's presence, were painful to her. She had evidently decided to take no further part in the talk. She looked restless and impatient, her eyes mutinous as they brooded out over the village, the church tower on the crest of the slope, and the smoke-deadened skyline with its jagged teeth of stacks and refuse, more of which was disclosed at every step through the widening gap between the village and the clay-dump. The end of the dune was not visible, since it curled back around the pit in a semi-circular wedge, and where it began to curve away from the road, leaving the surface clear of sand, an old winder-house stood facing the open downs — an oblong building with a black corrugated-iron roof and large windows, some of which were broken and boarded up.

Joe pointed past this erection, across the moor to a dark smudge of trees, tiny behind the pyramidal dumps, about two miles to the north.

'That's the grounds o' Beale's manor — daresay you've seen it close quarters by this time.' He spoke hesitantly, aware of Bronwen's reaction, yet fascinated and impelled, wishing to shake Mr Reed out of his complacency. 'Potter's house is miles further off, across the river, though 'tis said the shining roof of it can be seen in fine weather from Priory Bridge down by Tredoggett.'

The vicar turned, moistening his thin lips as he gazed curiously back along the valley. There was no sign of a river, but the heavy clay soil threw up several knots of woodland to the south-east.

'How long have Beale and Potter been known in the district?' he enquired.

'Years before I was born,' replied Joe. 'Nobody's sure where they came from, but they wasn't reared in Cornwall. There's a tale that says Beale arrived one night when there was a mutiny in Helburn clay-pit, Beale's oldest one across the river. 'Tis a secret pit with barbed wire fences all round — said to be worked by the inmates of the asylum close by. Beale used to be governor there, but soon after the riot he settled at the manor and started to govern us instead: got a grip on the clayworks and began buying up land from Potter's agents.'

The trio had reached the last sandbank, and the vicar stepped out with relief upon the clear road.

'Was Potter at the manor before Beale took it over?' he asked.

'No; his chief agent lived there for a time, but he'd cleared out and left the place empty while Beale was still at Helburn. It seems Beale swindled all Potter's agents — made the fellow mad when he found how they'd bungled everything. Beale's done the industry a lot o' good, there's no denying that — put in modern machinery and opened new pits. He's boss of all the clayworks within five miles now, while Potter's been hiding as long as I can mind — everything going against him.'

'He still owns some land in the valley, I believe?'

'One or two farms and woods around Tredoggett and a few lanes — one in particular called Potter's Lane. But most of it is waterlogged and the lanes is so narrow that they're never used by traffic: and they aren't lovers' lanes either — haven't been for ages.'

'Why not?'

Joe paused by the hedge to knock some mud off his boots.

'Well, there've been rumours,' he said looking fixedly at Mr Reed and lowering his voice. 'Potter seems to have a grudge against courting couples — threatens penalties to any who make free on his land. And the penalties may be pretty stiff. Ten year ago a Carn Veor couple was found drowned under Priory Bridge. It may have been a accident, o' course, but some people think Potter might have to face a few questions from Constable Rodda if he showed his nose in Carn Veor again.'

The vicar stared, feeling the tenseness, the threat of something uncanny and sinister breaking upon him through Joe's words, a power that he had already felt brooding among these clay-dumps, barbaric and offensive to his cultured mind.

'After a thing like that,' Joe continued, 'you can understand young folk not risking any more spooning in the woods. Potter don't seem to mind people trespassing as long as they're alone. Bronwen sometimes takes a short cut through his fields when she wants to hurry back from work, and she's never been molested. But if I was with her we'd keep to the main road for fear we too might be found under Priory Bridge next morning.'

Mr Reed shivered. He was evidently trying to dismiss Joe's tale as either a deliberate fabrication or a product of village superstition; yet the sense of malignant mystery in the general atmosphere and movement of the district oppressed him still.

Joe noted the vicar's perplexity and roused himself for another thrust of malicious humour.

'You'll hear more about these queer doings this afternoon when you see Beale,' he said. 'There's only one

19

reason why he'd want to rope you in, and that's to help him fight Potter.'

'Indeed!' The vicar was embarrassed by Joe's bluntness.

'That's the length of it, sir. And while Beale's trying to get favours from you I'll be trying to get a pretty big favour from Potter . . .'

'I've told him about that,' Bronwen put in quickly.

'Yes, Miss Cundy mentioned that you'll be approaching Mr Potter today with a view to getting employment. I trust you will be successful.'

Joe made no reply; he looked tense and turned aside on the pretext of adjusting a leaking tap outside the winder-house. As Bronwen also halted he let the water flow over his hands for a few moments, washing off the clay stains, then wiped them dry with his big red handkerchief.

The vicar noted the hint and was relieved by it; young people of this sort — crude individualists, poised in derision of all he stood for — were not to his taste. He had murmured a word of farewell and, quickening his steps, passed on towards the village.

Joe and Bronwen remained by the tap until he turned the bend and was hidden by the school playground wall, then linked hands and slowly followed him.

Chapter Two

THE outer street of the village was a drab, muddy stretch of road, without a pavement, sloping uphill to the north. There was about a score of dwellings on each side of it — all workmen's cottages with thick granite walls, small windows and low slate roofs. They were not arranged neatly, but with the maximum of disorder and variety of position. Several detached houses at ground level were followed by blocks of half a dozen, elevated from the road, then the farmyard of a smallholding, and beyond this a few cottages standing at right angles to the road, with alley-like spaces between them leading out to the clayworks. A grocery store stood by itself opposite the farmyard, its doorway reached by a flight of rough steps. Most of the dwellings had front gardens, some of them colourful with flower-beds — tulips, stocks and lilies already in full bloom — others used in more practical fashion for the growing of vegetables. All the shadows on the street were harsh, cast by stone or slate, unrelieved by the soft feathery shade of trees, though scattered elms and hawthorns could be seen above the roofs, slightly west of the village.

Joe and Bronwen moved haltingly around the corner by the school, walking a little apart and swinging their clasped hands like children. They knew that in every house where they were glimpsed nods would be exchanged, necks craned; women would rise from chairs, screen themselves behind curtains and watch as long as the couple were in sight. This was a common practice in Carn Veor, not specially directed at Joe and Bronwen. There was a pagan curiosity about these villagers,

21

surrounded as they were by the stark erotic landscape with its stiffened white breasts and slimy clay-beds. The scene was not merely industrial; the general whiteness and nakedness of the dunes and pits were massive symbols that dwarfed and distorted the normal approach to human passion. The carnal interest was raw and furtive, overshadowed by a sense of menace.

Joe and Bronwen had other worries at present. Joe was frowning at the school as they passed the broad iron gate of the playground. Nothing he had learned under that double-peaked roof had equipped him for the sort of life he was destined to live, or had any bearing upon his forthcoming approach to an employer.

Joe had been the type of boy whom the schools find most difficult to handle. He was incapable of concentration or study; he possessed no reliable talent, nothing that could be continuously reached and nourished. He picked up knowledge as he responded to experience, in random flashes, by intuition rather than intelligence. Yet his thought was not original or creative; he showed little imagination except in moments of heightened consciousness when, under the stimulus of happiness or expectancy, his mind flashed with the quaint, grotesque imagery of Celtic inheritance. Normally he perceived only the obvious; his peculiarity lay in the fact that he perceived it by those oblique movements which in a more profound mind would have resulted in original thinking. He belonged to the class loosely described as dreamers, but there was seldom anything romantic or poetic about his dreams; they were as harsh and grey as the sand-dunes, so that his mental world was limited, bounded by jagged horizons and smoky haze, through which a sudden white glare of illumination might pierce to glint on stagnant water. This mentality, combined with ill-health, had made him unemployable. He lacked the agile brain required for office work, he would have been an inefficient muddler as a shop assistant, and until recently he had not been physically strong enough for manual labour.

Bronwen had known him, and to some extent understood him, ever since he left school, while she was a mere child dropping in casually at the Gools' home, as at other homes in the village. But gradually, after she turned fifteen, she had yielded to the piquant impulse to see what she could do with him. He held for her the peculiar charm of a lopsided personality. His prolonged isolation had given various twists to his nature, stunting it in some directions, but also leaving him intact for a spontaneous enjoyment of maturity. He had felt as he entered his twenties that he could never marry a woman of his own age. He had reached manhood unfettered, undisciplined by any sense of responsibility, and though physically adult he was psychologically adolescent still, even a child in some ways, with a child's petulance and obstinacy. It was natural that he should be attracted towards Bronwen — an incorrigible tease, though in a stubborn, smouldering manner, without the cheap vivacity that would have irritated him by its lack of sexual awareness. Bronwen was aware, but she communicated her desire through a wayward playful effrontery, that was irresistible and richly satisfying to him. The bond between them was rare; it seemed likely to be permanent if Joe obtained work. He was nearly ten years older than she, so the affair could not be regarded by either of them as an innocent childish flirtation, even though they spent whole hours romping on the sofa, or the hearthrug at Joe's home, kissing and tickling each other. They were simple, instinctive creatures, children of the clay, though not fully children of the soil: a distinction that must often be made in

23

considering the people of this locality. They were not conscious rebels against modern social customs, but enjoyed the freedom of those who have never been in contact with subtle or sophisticated life. And since they would settle in Carn Veor there was little fear of their being disillusioned, of awakening to find that life was not really so simple as this. In Carn Veor it actually was so simple: one could never feel socially maladjusted in the village, for despite Beale's efforts, there was still practically no social life to adjust oneself to.

But Joe and Bronwen could be sober on occasions; they were sober now as they strolled forward between the houses. Their encounter with Mr Reed had aggravated tensions which in any case they would have felt during this brief journey. They were entering upon their first real crisis; the wave was gripping, shaking them.

The girl broke a long silence as they passed beyond the school, keeping to the centre of the road.

'I saw Florrie Balker just now,' she observed tentatively. 'Came in shop down Tredoggett and bought a gown. I could tell something cunning and spiteful had brought her there, before she let out her news.'

'Something about her man again?' enquired Joe.

'Yes. Ed have left her at last. They had a squabble this morning and things came to a head. Balker walked out and was going to catch the ten o'clock train at St Petroc — going to London, so Florrie said. He took all his money, though he hasn't been able to save much: he'll have to get a job right away up there to keep himself off the gutter. Haven't you heard about it in the village?'

'No; I've been out around the downs since breakfast time and ha'n't talked to anybody before you and Reed came along. But I aren't surprised. It had to

24

come to it. Balker and Beale never got on together. Ed didn't like Beale's funny little ways, though he'd owed everything to Beale since his parents died down Tredoggett.'

'True,' said Bronwen. She paused, her face clouded and puckered as she met Joe's eye. 'Queer what Beal had in his mind to choose that boy more than another and bring him back to live in the manor. Only eight or nine year old then, and Florrie the same age.'

Joe kicked at a lump of clay in the road, but the spell was upon him, holding his mind rigid.

'There was wickedness in it from the start,' he muttered tensely. 'Beale wanted to make sure Florrie didn't marry some swank from the towns who could score off her father. He made the chap go to claywork from the time he left school.'

'Yes; and when Florrie was — just my age — she and Ed was married in Carn Veor church, though 'tis said Potter did everything he could to make Ashford bar the doors against 'em.'

'It've been a fishy business all along,' Joe commented. 'Folks'll be minded afresh now o' the way Florrie came here among us, and there'll be fear stirred up in some o' the older ones who mind it. Both Beale and Florrie may be out for revenge now Ed have gived 'em the slip.'

Bronwen was breathing in gusts, watching her feet and Joe's leaving muddy tracks on the rough ground.

'I felt a bit fluttery this morning,' she confessed, 'when I saw that maid come in shop — standing there in her white fur coat, thin in the belly and with her green eyes and big flashing teeth. Like a hungry young wolf — as if she was hardly human, I felt, but might be — something *different* from us.'

Joe grunted, struggling to break through into practical, personal affairs, but pushed back by the knowledge that discussion even of these meant now a facing up to the monstrous, inhuman background.

'Florrie've took on some of her father's dark ways,' he said. 'But she's flesh and blood as much as we: Bert Truscott knows that well enough.'

'Still,' persisted Bronwen, ''tis a mystery where she came from. She wasn't born there in the manor any more than Ed; there hasn't been a woman there in living memory. All that's known is that Beale left Carn Veor — some say for a month or two and others think 'twas over a year — and suddenly turned up with a little maid. He let 'em all know 'twas his daughter.'

'But he wouldn't tell where he'd been,' said Joe. 'Folks reckoned 'twas across the river. He must ha' been with a woman anyhow.'

Bronwen's eyes groped into Joe's again, and she shivered.

'I've heard he keeps a wife over there, locked up in the asylum behind Helburn Pit.'

'Queer things was said to happen here too while Beale was gone,' remarked Joe. 'Father do mind it: he was telling of it only a night or two ago as we sat around the fire. Old Sam Nance, Rosa's grandfather, started a scare when he went up on the moor rabbiting one evening and came home wi' the tale that he'd seen the footprints of a wolf in the snow there where the woods end, and heard a wolf howling down by the water. Sam had travelled foreign and knew that no dog or fox could have made they footprints.'

Bronwen looked at a terrier that had trotted into the road ahead of them. She looked at it fearfully, as if expecting some uncanny transformation to take place. She had passed into a remote, topsy-turvy mood in which the most innocent objects became without reason

26

a source of swift-pouncing terror. She remained silent, and Joe resumed.

'Madness took hold o' many here in Carn Veor. Some was crazed with a new sort o' happiness and went around the lanes singing and ranting about Potter. But wi' most 'twas fear, and they kept all day at their bedroom windows that faced towards the manor and the roads leading away north over the moor, afraid o' the way Beale would show hisself when he came back. 'Twas war-time and there was few men left in Carn Veor to defend the place if Beale was training a pack o' wolves to scent out and kill all who held to Potter's side.

''Twas a hard winter, so father said, snowing week after week, and by nights the folk would bolt themselves in and look out over the snow and watch for the coming o' the wolves, or for a light to shine in Beale's house, showing he was home again.'

'And what was seen?' asked Bronwen.

'No wolves; but strange doings was in the manor at that Christmas time when Beale was in hiding. There was lights in the windows, but not Beale's lights; 'twas more like a searchlight and streamed up across the clouds and across to the houses here.' Joe pointed along the street, subdued and fear-ridden, as if he too expected some manifestation, and half desired it as a sign, strengthening him for the venture he was soon to make.

'Every one of our folks felt,' said Joe hoarsely, 'that when the light was thrown upon a house everything what was happening inside could be seen from the manor.'

'Who was it there?' murmured Bronwen.

A grim little laugh escaped Joe.

'Father's view is that old Potter had got in somehow. And they singing, ranting fools thought he'd drove

27

Beale off for good and got control o' Carn Veor at last. But they had a nasty shock — and Potter did too if that was his hope; for when Beale came back wi' the baby in the spring the people flocked to him; a great wave o' relief went through the village; and as the maid growed he was more popular and had more power over us than ever before.'

Bronwen nodded, shrinking from distasteful memories.

'He made her a favourite in all the concert parties here to Carn Veor, with her singing and dancing,' she said, 'and in St Petroc and Tredoggett too. But that wasn't all. She had a way wi' men that no other maid in the village — not even Rosa Nance — have shown so young. Or so I've heard dad say.'

'Yes, I remember,' said Joe dreamily. 'I went to school with her and I mind how scared Mr Teague was of her when she got to be a big girl of twelve or so. Scared o' the way she'd make sheep's eyes at him, I mean. She poisoned the school: Beale's power came through her plain enough, and we all felt it and was glad when she left.'

Chapter Three

JOE roused himself, drawing his cap lower as he glanced up at the sun.

'I wonder what'll be her next move,' he said with uneasy casual gliding towards personal issues. 'Did she drop any hint down Tredoggett just now?'

'No; but I felt she'd come in shop because she knew I'd be there. All the time she was talking I felt she was jeering at me, and had something up her sleeve.'

'Nothing for us to worry about. She'd never turn on *me* next.'

'Perhaps not in that way; but this scandal won't do us any good. People'll say we started indoors as bad as Ed and Florrie, and that our affair'll break down too — without getting as far as a wedding.'

'They've been saying that for months already. And all such talk'll be finished if I — if I'm lucky this afternoon.'

Bronwen caught her breath, releasing Joe's hand as she bent her head towards his. The doorway of the house they were passing was open and she dropped her voice almost to a whisper.

'You're going through with it, Joe? Not going to back out?'

'Not likely! There's too much at stake — and no other opening. Beale's clayworks mostly need skilled labour: there'd be no chance for me there, even if . . .'

Bronwen had flinched — a sign that Joe understood and that warned him vaguely of danger. Amid all the hard competent buoyancy of Bronwen's nature was a dark irrational vein — a fear almost amounting to terror, of Beale, and particularly of his hands. This had first become conscious to her last summer when he had chosen her to be carnival queen at the annual church fête. She had escaped on that occasion, and he had not yet crowned her, but she still lived in dread of him, of some new favour by which she might be entrapped. And along this duct of dread strange intimations reached her at times — intimations of the confused, dimly-flickering strife behind the common happenings of the village. Frightening questions nagged at her. Why had Beale wished to crown her with flowers? And why, when she fled from him on the day of the fête, meaning to hide in Potter's Lane, had she entered the wrong lane and come upon the carcase of a horse, half eaten away by rats under a clump of beech trees, and beside it a well full of clayey water that was stained with the blood of the dead horse? She seldom spoke to Joe of these matters, for they led into regions of the spirit which he had never penetrated. He had no especial fear of Beale, though he distrusted him and shared the general perplexity as to Beale's character and aims.

Bronwen rallied, staring past Joe at the farmhouse.

'You're sure you feel strong enough for Potter's work?' she enquired anxiously.

Joe squared his shoulders; his face had an odd expression, a doggedness through which he was trying to force jollity.

'I put in some practice on the sandbanks just now,' he said. 'Piled up the barrier for an hour, and didn't get any coughing or wheezing. I believe the asthma's cleared off for good.'

'I hope so. You'd need plenty o' breath to walk to Potter's farm every day. You'd have to get a bike if your job was across the river.'

''Twouldn't be there,' replied Joe, again shrinking.

'Even if he offered me work there I'd turn it down. Father says nobody in Carn Veor have worked across the river for twenty years. Potter's rules got more and more cranky and the work more and more danger-ous . . .'

Bronwen frowned moodily, entering the shadow with him. Their grip on commonplace reality was slipping, the prosaic nerve fading out to numbness.

'It's safe enough this side,' she observed with strained tenacity. 'Harry Rickard's been working around Tre-doggett fields since Potter took him on, carting manure. You might be wanted there with him, working with horses.'

'I don't care what 'tis as long as it don't mean crossing the river. There's only one bridge across it apart from Priory Bridge, and they was never used by the workmen on Potter's land. They fellows used to go over by ferry, so I've heard, landing where the river's dark under the trees and there's an old burial ground sloping down to the water. The ruins of a nunnery there — said to be haunted . . .'

The vision had flashed upon Joe's mind, startling him with the shudder of vague undercurrents. For a moment he almost touched the mood that had led Bron-wen to flee from the hands of Beale. But the flash spent itself without kindling a full awareness; he recoiled to an aggressive male stolidity, defiant.

'I aren't taking any risks even to get work to marry you. I'll lay down me own terms to Potter hisself. I shall ask for work around Tredogett where I can look over to the village and think o' you there in the shop, wi' nothing to mind me o' Potter's ferry and they buried nuns, or his funny doings across the river.'

They were now nearing the end of the street and were still the only persons in it. Most of the cottagers were

31

still at dinner, and the men who had returned from the morning shift at the clayworks were lounging about indoors.

But not far from the corner, on the left-hand side, there was a vivid break in the lifeless monotony of the row. To Joe and Bronwen it was a familiar sight, yet they looked, fascinated, seeing Joe's quest again on the human, practical level.

In the garden of the last detached house, screened from them until now by other dwellings, a wiry little woman with a sack tied round her waist was busily shovelling out a drill for potatoes. Her husband, a large, sleepy-looking man, leaned against the doorpost, watching her approvingly and drinking tea from a cup. The woman worked with gusto; she would frequently stoop and unearth a rotten potato that remained in the ground from last year's crop, and toss it back to the path. Her face, shown in sunlight when she straightened, was not an old one, and it was not too much creased; it had the battered look of a cannon ball, hard and shining, as if the skin drawn tightly over its bones had been polished. Strangely enough the face expressed contentment, even glee.

Bronwen greeted her as she and Joe drew abreast of the gate.

'Good afternoon, Mrs Yelland.'

The woman turned briskly, spade in hand, nodding.

'Good afternoon, both of 'ee!' She jerked a black thumb towards the doorway, her false teeth bared in a grin. 'See him there sticked up, warming his innards while I do his gardening for'n!'

'He ought to be ashamed of himself,' remarked Bronwen, speaking awkwardly, but released from the stifling mental atmosphere that had clouded her since she entered the village.

32

Yelland was not perturbed by her criticism. He drank noisily, his red fat face swelling and crinkling above the cup, as if he suppressed laughter. He shifted against the jamb, and having finished drinking he surveyed with mild and genial contempt the pair in the roadway.

'No good slinging mud,' he drawled, 'when you'm in the same fix yourself. Look at Joe there: mooning round the sand-burrows while you do the bread-winning down Tredoggett. Nothing wrong wi' me,' Yelland insisted, glancing blandly at a potato that came bouncing from his wife's hand almost to his feet. ''Tis over around the corner that things need to be put straight. Folks aren't blind, y'know, here to Carn Veor.'

Joe and Bronwen flushed, and the girl turned at once to Mrs Yelland with a question that answered her husband while suitably ignoring him.

'Joe's taking your advice — about applying to Potter for a job. You're sure it *is* genuine?'

Mrs Yelland patted the earth vigorously with her spade, as if all doubt of the matter had been buried with the potatoes.

'Potter's servant told me herself,' she said, tossing the words back over her shoulder in a loud rasping voice, 'that Potter could hardly get enough men to carry on his work proper, and would be glad if I could get any chaps to apply. There's no snag about it. Joe'll be earning his wages next week if he goes to Potter in the right way.'

Joe's face cleared; he was surveying the church tower, dark and barbaric in its mastery of the hilltop, though blurred by chimney smoke from the upper street of the village. The unearthly spell was broken; he was thinking of his marriage, the possible, solid fact within the walls of the church. The thought held him silent with its slow rousing of possessive heat towards Bronwen, and for a moment he dared not look at her.

Mrs Yelland resumed shovelling, but she had not finished her speech.

'I've been spreading the news around Carn Veor,' she went on jerkily, 'but none of the chaps don't seem to be interested. They think the servant was pulling my leg, or they fancy I dreamed everything that happened in Potter's Lane last Sunday; or else they got jobs already up at Beale's clayworks.'

Joe glanced back at Yelland, who, having dropped his cup on the doorstep, was complacently lighting a cigarette.

'Fact is,' said Joe bluntly, 'after all we've heard o' Potter we can't feel sure he's to be trusted. But as I've told Bron, I'm willing to take your word for it and give him a fair trial.'

'I should hardly put it that way, Joe: 'tis you who'll be on trial, not Potter. And I wish you'd both gone along to Potter's Lane before making this venture. I've been telling everybody 'tis the main thing . . .'

Bronwen raised a hand impatiently and took a decided step towards the corner.

'Sorry we can't stay to hear about that now,' she said quickly. 'Joe's got to hurry in for dinner and change, or he won't be home before dark.'

They moved on, and Mrs Yelland watched them, her face becoming shadowed, pitying. As they disappeared she screwed about towards her husband and shook her head ominously . . .

Joe and Bronwen were now in a wider street, though a very short one, upon which a road leading past the church opened at the northern end, and another hedged in westward near the corner. In the middle of this wide street, locally known as the Square, stood a granite war memorial — a cross with three steps at its base, around which a few children were playing, today being Saturday. Bronwen lived here in a cramped, four-roomed house, one of a block exactly opposite the monument. Joe's home was in the street beyond, almost under the shadow of the church.

Before moving on to the Cundy's dwelling Joe and Bronwen halted and looked back. They were on higher ground now, relieved by glimpses of the broader landscape. Above the roofs on the southern outskirts they saw the beacon rising in a bare low arc like the rim of a green moon, upon which the shaggy, potent blobs of the goats fidgeted within the small range of their tether. Eastward the new gravel cone of Carn Veor claywork loomed up with its gallows-like tip-beams smudged against the ridge of the old rambling dump where the landslide had occurred. The clatter of waggons on the tracks and the puffing of the winder-engine continued rhythmically, reminding them of the ceaseless mauling of soil, the ubiquitous purgation. But they seemed to be detached from it because of the fresh twist Mrs Yelland had given to their inner preoccupations. They were apart, mere spectators, observing and listening to alien movements. It was as though this activity under Beale's control were not self-existent, but simply a reflection and echo of something older, the will of Potter moving in a dark, secret lane. They were unpurged by that, outside Potter's land in all they did or desired, in the pride of their youth. They were stiffened against it, receiving the gross counterpart, the rasp of waggons, the flurry of white gravel spilled down between iron prongs in the sky.

Words came awkwardly now at parting. Bronwen said at length: 'You must be sure to call in, Joe, on your way home.'

'Of course.'

'I shall make a mess o' baking, I'm afraid, keyed up so much all the afternoon.'

35

'You mustn't worry. It'll be good news all right.'

'I feel sure o' that too. Potter must be hard up for workers, or the servant wouldn't have mentioned it. And we might have guessed it, for we know there's nobody in Carn Veor working for Potter except Harry Rickard.'

Joe's eyes probed hers starkly: he knew she was not thinking of Potter exclusively as an employer. His mind gripped the remoter aspect suggested by Mrs Yelland.

''Tis a funny business,' he said in a strained undertone, 'how that woman've been talking so much o' Potter lately, and how she's so different. I mind her getting wild with her man because he was so lazy and turned all the dirty work off on she.'

'I remember too,' Bronwen agreed, scanning with renewed fascination the beacon on which Beale had meant to crown her. She had a brief vision of it as it had been on that day of the fête when it was learnt that she had disappeared: the malevolent defiance of Beale running like an evil flame through the crowds. She felt herself drawn back, sucked down again into the vortex of conflict.

'And you've heard — we all have,' she resumed in a subdued, almost an awed voice, 'the reason Mrs Yelland gives for the change that's come over her. She'd have told it all over again if we hadn't broken away. She — she must have been driven last Sunday as I was — at the time of the carnival. But she found the *right* lane.'

'She took her directions from Potter's guide-book, it seems,' replied Joe indifferently. 'You didn't do that!'

'No; it was just . . . I was just scared, that's all, afraid o' Beale touching me. I minded that the year before when he crowned Elsie Spry he leaned over and kissed her cheek, and everybody was laughing about it. But they Sprys didn't laugh when they found Elsie hanging dead in the wash-house last Easter.' Bronwen shuddered.

'Don't let's talk o' they things,' Joe put in. He glanced uncomfortably at the children, who were watching him and the girl furtively as they played around the memorial. 'I know we got to think o' Potter now, and you can't think of him without dragging in Beale too. But let's look on the bright side.' He paused a moment, forcing a grin.

'I see things fitting in pretty well to celebrate our success tomorrow. You know we're having visitors?'

'Your cousin Gregory and his girl?'

'That's it. We've ordered a fowl o' George Gumma — mother's gone over for it by this time, I expect. And I fancy that fowl'll do something more than give Gregory another bone to pick. "Three cheers for Potter!" I'll be saying when she's put on the dinner table. "He's a kind-hearted old buffer after all." And you'll be feeling the same in there wi' your father.'

Bronwen freshened, smiling as she stepped forward to the gate of her home and lifted the latch.

'You can come in,' she said with a flash of her normal teasing intimacy, 'just for a minute in the passage. Dad isn't back from work yet.'

Joe followed her silently into the house.

Chapter Four

TIMOTHY CUNDY halted his bicycle on the stone bridge over the mineral railway that cut across the landscape about a mile north of Carn Veor. He set his foot on the wire fence that was attached to the parapet, guarding the steep slope to the track, and lit a cigarette, the smoke curling up past his close-clipped ginger moustache, and around the peak of his clay-smeared cap as he bent his head low over the match to shield its flame from the wind.

The bridge crested a squalid stretch of road, flanked on the east by rambling stone heaps from quarries. Huddled under these were a pair of tumble-down cottages and a derelict drying-shed whose broken stack rose from a dense growth of bramble by the roadside. A hundred yards from the base of the bridge another cottage overlooked a small clay-pit that had been long abandoned and was half full of oozing mud-banks and discoloured water. But to Timothy, who had no eye for beauty, there was nothing repellent in this industrial ugliness. As he straightened up, his gaze slipped indifferently over it, his aggressive clay-powdered face absorbed by more arresting details in the distance.

From this vantage-point both Carn Veor and Beale's manor were visible — the village gaunt and bare on the southern skyline, the manor, a mile to the north-west, softened a little by its screen of trees. Timothy viewed Beale's home with an intentness which showed that it possessed a new, personal fascination for him. He had learnt from the workmen who had arrived to take the next shift as he left Henstone clay-pit that Balker had at last gone from the manor. The news gave him a peculiar satisfaction, a sense that things were moving in the direction he had long awaited. After two years as a widower he was becoming restless, hungry, especially now that Bronwen had grown up and revealed in her mastery of Joe some of the hard sensual heat she inherited from her father. He had been a faithful husband, but was not without a certain streak of brutality that made his virtue precarious after his wife's death.

He sat there in the sun and brooded, puffing at his cigarette, his small, rather bloodshot eyes glowing as they swept the environs of the manor. He seemed to be watching for a signal, contemplating the crucial step, assured that his powers were adequate. There was a touch of arrogance about him, and this was his normal characteristic; he had a massive pride in himself, a supreme contempt for all other wills — even Beale's. It was not from him that Bronwen had derived her strange terror of the claywork master; this was the one trait in her which he found incomprehensible and despised. Physically, and in her emotional texture, she owed much to him — her tall bony figure, her ginger hair, her big muscular hands, and the stubbornness of her unyielding spirit. Timothy was a superb specimen of mature manhood, heavy and towering, with the hint of the bully in his general look and bearing — particularly his voice, for he bawled and shouted the most trivial remarks, and scarcely ever laughed. He was a dour, truculent materialist, and though he had worked for Beale for twenty years he regarded him as an equal rather than a master.

Timothy shifted around on his seat and peered ahead towards Carn Veor. His thoughts also shifted somewhat, striking another aspect of the situation that engrossed him. Bronwen would be back from Tredoggett by now; probably Joe was with her. The idea was not displeasing to Timothy, though he could have wished that she had chosen a more virile and competent lover. But her relation with Joe had at least brought a piquant tang of scandal into his domestic life. His moral conscience was not greatly developed. As long as Bronwen was talked about and looked at with carnal curiosity, he was content. The gossip about her behaviour in Joe's bedroom did not offend him. It reminded him that he was the father of a powerful female creature, and this appealed to his primitive pride. He had no doubt of her virtue, but recently he had become anxious that the affair should lead to practical and permanent results. He wanted the pair to marry, and sometimes spoke to Bronwen in a suggestive manner which she resented. On the whole, however, there was little friction in the Cundy's home. It lacked the placidity of the Gools', its atmosphere was more raw and potentially explosive, but there were few squabbles between Timothy and his daughter. Each respected the hard, unrefined vitality of the other, each was thick-skinned, insensitive to the subtleties of domestic tension, and Bronwen's tomboy spirit enabled her to take Timothy's blusterings in her stride, even laugh at them with an elusive audacity that Timothy really admired.

He scanned the cluster of dunes beside the village, and was about to resume his homeward journey when his attention was arrested. A plume of smoke had heaved up behind the white ridges, rising slowly and ominously like a signal. He knew at once that it did not proceed from the stack of a drying-kiln; it was thicker and seemed to be streaked with a dull glow, a reflected radiance that was not a trick of the sunlight glittering on the sand. Timothy watched, puzzled and expectant, stiffened on the saddle and gripping the wire fence with rigid concentration. The glare fanned up higher along the root of the smoke-cloud, tingeing it more ruddily; the cloud spread towards the village, dwarfing the gravel dumps and the houses.

Timothy soon realized what had occurred, but showed no particular shock or surprise. Like the other villagers he had grown accustomed to these manifestations, and accepted them as inevitable, expressions of the warfare that raged in the district, the conflict between the flesh and the spirit, the yielding and recoil of weak, unguarded natures.

'Another o' Rosa's fires, by the look of it,' he muttered. 'And in Carn Veor itself this time. She must ha' done her work pretty close to home last night wi' somebody. Wonder who 'twas, wonder?'

Stimulated by curiosity on this point he cycled on down the slope of the bridge and on to the flat, hedgeless road winding through the downs beyond. And while he pedalled vigorously towards the blaze there came increasing signs that it had already been observed in the village and that the usual commotion had broken out. A black saloon car glided past him, and he caught a brief glimpse through its window of the taut, smouldering face of Beale, who had been summoned by telephone from the manor. Other cars flashed by, and as Timothy ascended the ridge behind Carn Veor he heard the clanging bell of a fire engine away to the west, and saw in the sunlight the glittering red machine, pulling a trailer behind it, racing along the road from St Petroc into the village. It emerged from the Square, passed the church and swerved down the claywork lane.

Within a few minutes he, too, had reached the head of the lane, where a drab two-storey office had been erected on the corner. He turned the bend and cycled on down a raised cinder-track that was laid through the

41

fields, leading into the fold of the curving dunes. Down there in the hollow, shielded by the gravel heaps, were the main claywork buildings — the drying-sheds, engine-houses, and store-rooms, and the blocks of tanks and micas at the pit-heat.

As he came in sight of the actual blaze Timothy saw that it was the old engine-house that was on fire — a tall grim structure with thick granite walls and a rusty bobbin-frame projecting below its peaked slate roof. It had not been active as an engine-house for some years; the windows were boarded up and the interior used for storing oil, timber and tools. A small winder-house at the rear contained all the machinery for drawing up the wagons, while the pumping engine was installed in a new engine-house on the other side of the clay-pit.

The broad square between the drying-sheds and the edge of the concrete tank basin was a scene of feverish activity when Timothy entered it round the high wall of the coal-yard. The fire-engine had been drawn up under the sand-dump, the trailer standing on the verge of the parapet a dozen yards away, at the top of a flight of steps leading down to the long rows of tanks. Firemen were unloading the sections of hose from the trailer, connecting them in a snake-like coil stretching down the whole length of the steps and across the flat outer side-walk between the big square pools. The inner sidewalk could not be approached because of falling ash and debris from the engine house looming directly above it. The tiny darting figures of the firemen were blurred by the smoke-clouds; the hot ragged waves of flame licked out towards them through the gored windows, roaring and crackling in their unchecked and rapidly spreading grasp of the building. Other firemen stood by the engine, awaiting the moment to release the jets from the connected hose. They eyed the burning structure

42

gloomily, shaking their heads; there was obviously no hope of saving it. All that could be done was to prevent the fire from reaching the more valuable winder-house.

When Timothy dismounted from his bicycle and left it propped against the coal-yard wall, he was one among at least a dozen villagers arriving on the scene. Men and women were forming groups along the back of the enclosure, children racing about, pointing and chattering excitedly.

Timothy strode forward and halted just behind the trailer. He was not a sociable man and was in no mood to gossip with the other spectators. He waited, detached and critical, frowning over his cigarette.

At last the pumps throbbed into action and a fierce steady jet of green water slapped through the back window of the engine-house. Slates began falling from the roof as some rotten rafters were burnt through, and the flames leapt vertically up through the holes, bursting out amid a great flurry of smoke with almost the force of an explosion. Water continued to drive and splash into the heart of the blaze, running among the oil drums and spilling over the wooden stairway that had for years been suspended against the inner wall, its bottom half cut away to make room for storage. But the fire raged on unabated, the smoke poured out through the windows, the roof and the doorways, so that the whole scene became weirdly shadowed, the noises smothered and reverberating between the vaguely looming arc of clay-dunes. The firemen and even the spectators sweated in the intense heat.

Timothy watched in dour silence, his tongue between his teeth after he had thrown aside his fag-end. Human movements seemed dreamlike and unreal before this strange elemental conflict. He saw Beale standing with other claywork officials a few yards behind the fire engine, viewing the disaster with sphinxish, impassive countenance. Glancing in the opposite direction he noted that, at the mouth of the gully leading down to the clay-pit from the tanks, the claywork captain, Bill Rowse, was holding and questioning a boy of about ten. The boy seemed terrified and was evidently confessing what he knew about the origin of the fire.

Timothy's scowl deepened uneasily as he looked at them. Perhaps, after all, this incident was not fused with the mood in which he had left Henstone, the hot, carnal drive towards possession. Perhaps it was not Rosa's affair this time, but only some mischief-loving boy who had fired the oil drums.

Within a few minutes his suspicion was confirmed. Rowse led the boy, who had begun whimpering, up from the gully and across a trolley-line towards the group of officials. Several villagers pressed forward, and the captain nodded stiffly in response to their bewildered queries.

'Yes — it's his doing, I'm afraid.'

He dragged the boy across the enclosure to Beale, and the ensuing explanations were closely watched by those who were not still absorbed in the main drama at the engine-house. Beale shrugged indifferently, made impatient gestures with his long arms and soon dismissed the captain who retired rather sulkily and released the boy. As he did so Beale turned to the other officials, muttered a few brusque words of apology or farewell, and began moving with his odd shambling gait up the lane towards the office, where he had left his car.

When he had disappeared Timothy roused himself. He felt cheated of what had been essential to him in the present drama. He was aware of the old hunger, the lure of the manor, the prospect now open to him through the departure of Balker. He thought afresh of Bronwen and

Joe, and of the venture Joe was making to clear the way for his marriage to the girl. Settling thus back into his personal perspective, he took a last contemptuous survey of the clouded feverish scene, noting that the flames had been checked a little and were no longer breaking so fiercely through the window that overlooked the roof of the winder-house. He then spat and returned with a slow, deliberate tread to his bicycle.

'Fires isn't nothing unless 'tis the sort we'm used to,' he said grumpily to a neighbour who lounged against the wall. He pushed his bicycle away towards the clearer air of the field nearer the village.

When he reached the roadway and mounted his machine he saw that Beale was standing on the step outside the office door, watching the approach of a black-garbed figure — Mr Reed, who had just turned the corner by the Square, a hundred yards off.

'Bad luck, Mr Beale!' called Timothy as he cycled by.

Beale made no response. His personality seemed to be focussed with a strange malice and cunning upon the vicar, as though he was released from the petty irritation that had caused him to turn from the engine-house, fronting again massively the more potent and subtle danger, the destroyer at the heart of his clay-lands, the stroke from which this clerical figure might temporarily shield him. The ugly smile Timothy noted on his face was that of a man who had selected a victim . . .

Timothy passed the church, looked quizzically at the Gools' home as he drew abreast of it, and had soon turned into the Square and dismounted at his own gateway. He propped his bicycle against the window-sill, removed his muddy boots and put on the pair of shoes Bronwen had set by the door, and strode into the dark passage. The low roar of a primus stove in the kitchen told him that Bronwen was preparing a meal. He licked

45

his lips hungrily and entered the little room, his big feet slopping in the unlaced shoes.

Bronwen was laying the table as if for tea; she would cook a hot meal later in the afternoon. As Timothy came in and hung his cap to a nail in the beams, she glanced up from the dishes, her face rather flushed and agitated.

'I thought you'd be late in,' she greeted with a nervous laugh. 'Things livening up a bit, aren't they?'

Timothy took off his clayey coat and flung it over the stair-post.

'Heard about the fire?' he asked.

'Yes; we heard people outside who'd seen the smoke rising, before Joe left here. But we didn't take much notice: Joe's got other things to attend to this afternoon.'

'He went out over the sandbanks to meet 'ee, I s'pose?'

Bronwen nodded.

'We came in with the vicar,' she replied grudgingly. 'He'd been to Tredoggett — couldn't motor down because the road's blocked. He overtook me in the valley — a nuisance, as Joe was looking forward . . . But we made up for it a bit when we got in.'

'I bet you did,' grunted Timothy, eyeing her face somewhat gloatingly as she bent it while mechanically slicing bread.

After a pause she peered round at him, a little dazed, preoccupied with the memory of Joe's embrace, the farewell kisses and the shy way he had caressed her to strengthen himself out there in the dim passage.

'What's burning this time?' she enquired.

'Old engine-house.'

'Have they got it under control yet?'

'Started to as I left. They'll save the winder-house but no more. Got too strong a hold afore the fire-brigade got

46

there. Always the same wi' these fires. Beale ought to keep a fire-engine handy on every claywork if he want to save more than black walls on his landscape.'

Bronwen turned the screw of the primus stove on the table, as the kettle was boiling. The flame dwindled, the roar sank to a low hum, spluttered and ceased.

'Do you know — who did it?' Her voice sounded strained in the sudden hush.

A mirthless, grating laugh from Timothy echoed through the room. He lurched past the table, his large head, covered with short bristly ginger hair, poking into the full stream of daylight near the window.

''Tis a fair swindle this time,' he shouted. 'Neither Rosa nor man behind it so it seem — only Tucker's boy playing around wi' matches. We couldn't believe our senses when Rowse haled the kid fore to Beale. I'd ha' come straight home if I'd knowed that's all 'twas.'

Bronwen stared, incredulous also for a moment.

'H'm!' she commented then. 'This is rather innocent for a change!'

'Innocent! I should say 'twas!' cried Timothy. 'Anything so tame as this is a disgrace to a place wi' our reputation. The talk that come after the fires — that's what we relish most — when the man have been found and everybody's guessing what his wife'll do about it. There's a real kick in life for us while the rumours is coming in — some saying his missus have left him, others saying she've only give him a taste of her fist or the rolling-pin — or gone straight to Nances' to have it out wi' Rosa herself. That's the stuff we live on here at Carn Veor. 'Tis what we need pumped into us to keep our minds off the crazy doings in Potter's Lane. And this time we'm fooled.'

'P'raps the boy's covering up something,' murmured Bronwen.

47

'Maybe so. We shall be wiser about it before the week-end's gone. And about other things too.'

Mysterious hints of this sort were common in Timothy's speech, and Bronwen paid no attention to it except to cast him a sharp glance while filling the tea-pot.

Timothy closed the middle door and opened another behind it which gave entrance to a cellar, or 'spence' as the Cornish call it, under the stairs. Inside were brooms, enormous stone jars containing raw vegetables, pitchers with round slabs of slate covering their mouths, bottles, tins and brushes on shelves, saucepans and frying-pans hung from the stairs at varying levels and, facing the doorway, a bowl of water standing on a tripod.

It was Timothy's habit to give his face and hands a superficial streaming on his return from work, leaving the more thorough wash with soap and flannel until after he had taken a meal. He rolled up his shirt sleeves and thrust his huge hairy hands, with their thick powdering of dry clay, into the water.

Bronwen drew a chair from beside the dresser and set it at the table. She stood watching Timothy, carelessly flicking a few crumbs from her green pinafore.

'Me and Joe'll be settled all right this week-end — I feel sure o' that,' she murmured.

Timothy's reply was muffled in his wet hands as he ducked his head to the level of the bowl.

'I daresay he got good heart towards it at the moment. You'm a hot maid, Bron, and can put enough guts in a man to tackle Beale and Potter together if need be. Even such a wisht mortal as Joe must amount to something after you've fed him up. But all 'same, I wish he wasn't going to Potter.'

'There's nowhere else for him.'

48

'Don't be too sure o' that. He may rue the day, like Harry Rickard here next door.' Timothy straightened and turned, his eyes tightly shut as he groped for a towel hung on the door of the 'spence'. Having found it he whisked it off its nail and wiped his mouth. 'Harry's thinking to try Beale's again, so he've told me. Work like a slave's and wages to starve on, that's all he've got on Potter's farm.'

Bronwen stiffened, the old obstinacy clouding her face. 'I don't believe it. Mrs Yelland told us again just now . . .'

'You can't trust anything that woman's saying,' Timothy interrupted, speaking through the towel which still covered his face. 'She been cracked since last Sunday. Potter's Lane have done its dirty work on she.'

'Well, Joe's going to Priory Bridge anyway,' Bronwen stated. 'And p'raps you'll have to eat your words yet. We'll be married this summer on those starvation wages you talk of.'

'Reckon you'll have to be — even if you do starve,' retorted Timothy. 'Things isn't standing still because you chose a weakling or a fool for your partner.'

Bronwen frowned steadily at him with a hint of defiance, but her next remark was casual, seemingly irrelevant to their discussion.

'Ed Balker've made a big move — cleared out o' Beale's manor this morning — for good, so I hear.'

Timothy replaced the towel on its nail and strode towards her, his face glowing with a dark enigmatic sensuality.

'No news to me, maid. And I could tell 'ee more about that if I choosed. 'Tisn't only Joe what's looking for openings.'

Bronwen shrugged; she was puzzled, noting unusual excitement in Timothy's manner. But she was in no

49

mood to probe him further: though unsubtle, he could be fiercely and exasperatingly secretive at times. She evaded personal implications, and remarked lightly:

'Mrs Yelland's looking for openings — and finding plenty, by the look of it. She's stirring the whole village with her talk of — of what she saw in Potter's Lane.'

Timothy grunted derisively as he seated himself on the chair.

'There's one good thing this fire'll do, even if 'tisn't Rosa's,' he announced. ''Twill give a more healthy turn to the talk here. 'Tis as big a setback for Mrs Yelland as for Beale. We shan't hear no more about Potter's Lane this week-end. Claywork doings seem more natural to us somehow.'

Chapter Five

THE vicar had left his home in a state of bewilderment and incredulity. He had seen the smoke from the burning engine-house while taking lunch with his wife in the dining-room, and recalling Joe's recent words he was more than ever perplexed and shaken by the sense of something uncanny and abnormal in the affairs of the district. There was a suggestion of conspiracy, of feud and general upheaval which jarred upon his taste for serene contemplation. He had no clue to the enigma and tried to evade those undertones of mystery and to regard this outbreak as a mere accident, appealing to his curiosity and perhaps — if there were any loss of life — demanding his professional sympathy and interest. He hurried through the meal and rose, moving towards the hall for his hat and overcoat.

Mrs Reed — a tall, odd-looking woman with protuberant eyes and a long, dark, haggard face — was obviously distressed, staring fearfully at the spreading veil of smoke; she became almost hysterical as she heard the fire engine clang by outside the vicarage gate. A neurotic woman, furtive and tormented in her emotions, she let any suggestion of the morbid seize upon her nerves and nag her near to madness.

'Will you motor out to see Mr Beale now?' she asked in an awed, shuddering voice.

The vicar shook his head dubiously.

'It would be useless, I'm afraid. He'll be occupied with this disaster on the claywork.'

Mrs Reed looked strangely at her husband, her face

51

wrenched and fevered with excitement. Her hands clasped and knotted vaguely in the air.

'I do want you to meet Mr Beale, Felix. He is such a fascinating man. I'm sure he could do more than anyone else to get us settled in this dreadful district.'

'It's dreadful enough, certainly,' replied the vicar with a shrug of irritation. 'It seems to have killed Ashford in his prime — he was only forty-five. Such a strain as this — one crisis on top of another — would shatter the strongest constitution in a few years.'

'And yet Mr Beale seems a wonderfully robust man,' said Mrs Reed. 'He seems to *enjoy* it in some way. It's fascinating.'

'Well, I may see him at the works,' the vicar replied coolly, and a few minutes later he was moving down the drive, frowning and disquieted.

His wife's neurosis was a sombre domestic background against which he had been obliged to labour even amid the placid, healthy scenes of the rural parish near Saffron Walden, Essex, where he had spent the past ten years. The tension of this Cornish countryside, its dark carnal suggestiveness, was clearly aggravating the trouble. He had so far been unable to establish normal marriage relations with her at the Carn Veor vicarage. She had recoiled fiercely into herself, away from natural usage, as if she apprehended a new potency and expected some alien flash through her starved blood. The marriage had been childless and unhappy, both of them awaiting the elemental fire that would destroy the innate fastidiousness and reserve, the false delicacy, that estranged and deprived them. The vicar had little hope that the more primitive Cornish environment would release and stabilize them now amid the difficult adjustments of middle-age. He had loathed the clay landscape from the first moment he glimpsed it, and his deepening knowledge of it was forcing him into an acute spiritual disharmony. He was beginning to perceive the clay land as a sort of evil parody of the mental climate and texture which he found most odious — the climate and texture of orthodoxy. He disliked the industrial scene for the same reason that he disliked orthodox dogma — because it was a barbarous, arbitrary interference with the natural order of things. The whole area was in a continuous state of unrest. All day long the soil was suffering vicious assaults and transformations — blasted by dynamite, bitten into by excavators, washed under hose-jets and finally shaped by sheer mechanical force into hard white cubes. The entire process was horrifying in its suggestion of the spiritual parallel. Beliefs that came soothingly to the mind amid the unstained fields and woods were incongruous and unreal here. This was dogma's world — originally Potter's he had heard, though now controlled by Beale — and it loomed menacingly over the tranquil levels of meditation. From the oozing slime of its gored cliffs and the ruddy glare of its furnaces he caught a purgatorial idiom which filled him with alarm and self-distrust.

Mr Reed was a timid man, and his religious outlook reflected his timidity. He had renounced orthodoxy because he lacked the spiritual stamina to bear the incessant stress of its turbulent vitality. He disbelieved in miracles because he was too weary to grapple with such a complex universe as a belief in miracles would imply. He recoiled from the thought of Divine invasions of Nature, sudden injections of supernatural force which turned the world upsidedown. He shrank in squeamish protest from this burly energy that worked through shocks and explosions, and made its witnesses, from St Paul to Barth, so explosive and so shocking to the

53

civilized taste. He wished only to be left in peace on the purely human level where he could perfect his philosophy of the good life and help people to be nicer to each other. And he thought himself a courageous man in thus exchanging a fierce, stormy spiritual world for a snug and orderly one. It was only about his marriage that he was really honest; there he admitted that at least Mrs Reed's aversion to the full, rich vigour of living was a mistake.

He passed quickly through the village, aware of being an outsider with no clue to the mood of the people hurrying and chattering about him. Most of them glanced at him with suspicion, even resentment, as though he were an intruder upon some secret ritual which they would enjoy more freely without his presence. He murmured a few words in reply to greetings, but his round, dark face remained tense and aloof, unresponsive.

When he turned the corner and saw Beale standing on the office step he was sharply conscious of being in a kind of bottleneck, driven blindly forward by the pressure of his ignorance and need, groping towards the breadth and release which that hunched, powerful figure seemed to offer him. The burning engine-house faded into the background of his mind; he cast only a vague glance down across the fields to the red-veined smoke that belched from the building. He also ignored Timothy, who cycled past in dour silence. His eyes fastened on Beale with the assurance his wife had expressed just now — that only through Beale could he hope to become useful or acceptable in this parish.

Drawing near he studied with increasing fascination the personal appearance of the claywork master. Beale was rather short and round-shouldered, but strongly built, with long arms and very large hands that were rough and hairy as a labourer's, the two rings he wore on the little finger of his right hand looking incongruous on the coarse skin. His face was peculiar — a dark simian face in which some of the features warred with the general aspect and character. The obstinate cleft chin, the thin lips, the hook nose should, the vicar felt, have been completed by the flashing eyes and high forehead of the thinker. But the eyes, though they were round as a monkey's, were dull and blurred by opaque white spots on the cornea. They had a strange power, an intensity different in kind from that thrown out by an acute, rational mind: it was a sort of animal intensity, yet it had a darkly spiritual significance. His forehead was extremely low, slanting backward under a black bowler; the whole head seemed to have been pressed back and flattened, forming a bulge at the rear, overhanging the short neck. Altogether he gave the impression of being not so much a man of fine intelligence as a man of erratic creative power — dangerous because he could stand apart from his intellectual qualities, assessing them from a more primitive standpoint, using them with a spiritual cunning that lacked the innocence of an instinct. He was clearly a person whose energies were harnessed to a single aim, a man who could be ruthless or quixotically generous as he regarded each situation on its bearing on private plans that had no reference to the common ambitions of a capitalist. Yet the spell of his personality was sufficient to override his repulsive appearance. The most sensitive and refined spirits in the county valued, even depended upon, the guidance of this clouded and sinister force that moved among them, amiably for the most part, but releasing just that dark, elemental potency which they lacked.

Beale came down from the step and held out his hand as Mr Reed halted. His fingers quivered as he seized the thin, pale hand of the vicar; he bared his teeth in a smile.

'Mr Reed. I fancied you might come along to express your sympathy. A very different meeting from the one we had anticipated at the manor!'

The vicar flushed.

'I'm sorry to meet you under these trying circumstances, Mr Beale,' he replied. 'It seems incredible — if this is more than an accident . . .'

'Oh, it's more than that — though not quite the usual pattern. I find it's a trick played on me by my rascal of a son-in-law — through one of the village boys.'

'Indeed!' said the vicar, uncomprehending. 'I hope the damage is not extensive?'

Beale shrugged, jerking his arm towards the lane.

'I've just been down to look at it. The fire brigade will save what they can — not much I'm afraid.'

'Anyone injured?'

'Oh, no — merely the building, as usual. There's never any need of an ambulance after these fires . . . Were you going down to view the tragedy?'

'Well, I — er — I had intended . . .'

Beale raised his hand, resolved and peremptory.

'Come into the office for a few minutes: we can discuss the subject we intended to talk over at the manor. My colleagues will stay down by the engine-house until the firemen have finished their job.'

He pushed open the unlocked door and entered the bare little office. Mr Reed followed nervously. Passing a small private room Beale led the way into the main business room at the rear — a somewhat musty place, though well lighted by the big oblong window. Several tables, desks and chairs stood on the canvas-covered floor, but the modern office equipment, telephone and typewriters, seemed incongruous against the raw industrial background. The walls displayed maps of the clay district showing Beale's works as red blobs, graphs recording rise and fall of output, and photos of some of the pits.

The room was cold, but Beale did not switch on the electric fire: and as he was a non-smoker he could offer his guest no soothing narcotic. The atmosphere remained harsh, unrelaxed.

Beale moved to a table in the centre of the room and motioned the vicar to a chair beside it, facing the window. Beale sat down opposite, shifting his chair a little so that he, too, could view the clouded smouldering heart of the claywork. The sense of the drama proceeding at the engine-house gave a sharpness and urgency to Beale's mood. He did not waste time in preliminaries, but came straight to the topic he had wished to discuss with Mr Reed at his home that afternoon.

'And how do you like your new appointment?'

The vicar hesitated, clearing his throat before he replied, without looking at Beale:

'I — er — haven't had time to form a considered opinion as yet. I'm waiting for things to quieten down a bit and become — well, somewhat more normal.'

'You will need patience,' commented Beale drily. 'Things are fairly normal as they are — from our particular standpoint. It's something of a volcanic region, and you must be prepared for eruptions.'

'I expected Cornwall to be a little more primitive than Essex,' the vicar admitted. 'But it seems fantastic that the present state of affairs can be anything but exceptional even in a remote corner of a Celtic land.'

'It certainly has nothing to do with the people being Celtic,' said Beale. 'It may be simply that they are a trifle more human — more *nakedly* human — than their neighbours in East Anglia.'

Mr Reed smiled faintly.

57

'I could hardly agree with that,' he observed. 'The types I have met so far seem almost intractable — and not only the older generation. I was struck by the same quality an hour ago when I came across a young village couple — Joe Gool and Bronwen Cundy . . .'

'Ah, yes. That girl!' Beale bit his lip, brooding and reminiscent for a moment. 'You have her to blame for the deficit in the church finances last year.'

'Eh? In what way?'

'The annual fête. I chose her to be carnival queen, but somehow she became terrified of the prospect, and at the time when I should have been crowning her she ran off. The whole event was disorganized and — well, village passions broke out in a regrettable manner. We had to send out search parties, and one of them found her early the next morning asleep in one of the valley lanes.'

Mr Reed looked severe, and ventured a brief flash of self-assertion.

'She hardly seemed to me the type to choose for a carnival queen. Rather coarse and common — nothing attractive about her.'

'I had my reasons for choosing Bronwen Cundy . . . But let that pass. The important thing is that this leads into the heart of our discussion. It's not merely the girl you have to blame for that idiotic prank. I am quite sure that Potter had communicated with her in some way and suggested that she should wreck our effort on behalf of the church. You must be ready to meet setbacks of this kind. You can never tell by what means Potter will strike next. I do not wish to alarm you unduly, but I feel you should be warned at the outset that the religious and cultural life hereabouts can make headway only in the teeth of Potter's opposition.'

Mr Reed looked perplexedly into Beale's face as the

58

claywork master leaned across the table towards him.

'I've gathered something of this — Mr Potter's character,' he said.

'From the villagers?'

'Yes.'

'It's mere guesswork as far as they're concerned — except for those who have read his fantastic guide-book.'

'Does he never visit Carn Veor?'

'Not to my knowledge. But I've seen him here in the past. I well remember the last time, for his gestures then were obviously those of bafflement — gestures of grief and rage that confirmed my view that a changed emphasis must be expected in his future moves against me.' Beale straightened, rubbing his hands together, a new smouldering vitality was rising in him, subduing the vicar to silence, nonentity. His voice grew louder as he went on:

'It was oddly enough on the night Bronwen Cundy was born — a thundery summer night, almost tropical in its effect on the senses. The young folk of Carn Veor were enjoying themselves, happily innocent of Potter's presence. I alone saw that figure, mysteriously cloaked and hooded, dark as a lost spirit as it glided where it would and saw what it would. I trailed him wherever he went, but kept at a safe distance. He may have been armed, and he has violent moods; indeed he is suspected of having committed at least two murders . . . Perhaps you have heard?'

'Yes,' replied the vicar, drawn irresistibly into the hot sensual current that Beale was gradually releasing, 'Joe Gool mentioned it just now. A strange story: I regarded it as mere superstition.'

'Potter is more dangerous than you know,' commented Beale with a glint of malice in his blurred eyes.

59

'I could take no chances. But from a place of safety I watched him climb Carn Veor beacon as the thunderstorm approached, and stand on its summit, looking down over the village. He stretched out his arms, vainly entreating, and as his mutterings reached me I caught his words:

'"Ye shall lament for the teats, for the fields of desire, for the fruitful vine."'

Mr Reed edged back from the table, glancing quickly at the floor; his cheeks reddened. Beale, however, seemed to find no embarrassment in the revelation. He continued:

'Potter spoke these words with deep sadness and conviction. No doubt he really believed that in choosing to experience love as I allow, and as their own nature dictates, without regard to his fantastic rules, the people of these clay lands are forced at last to lament the dead years. He saw in his sombre mind how these pleasures tend to disillusion, the desire becoming choked with jealousy and disgust, the vine of womanhood languishing with the cooling of the blood and satiety. But the young lovers knew and cared nothing for his grief. And thinking of this he lifted his hand to the sky as if he would bid the heavens to weep with him; and indeed, just then the rainstorm began. But the downpour only drove the lovers to find shelter in the huts of my clay-works; some even entered the engine-house which is now burning. And seeing himself thus foiled at every point, he revealed to me his true character. Cruelty and vengeance darkened his face as he raised it, and while lightning flashed I heard him cry out in judgment:

'"Give them, O Lord, what wilt Thou give them? Give them a miscarrying womb and dry breasts."'

'With that biblical curse he turned away south towards Potter's Lane and the — mysterious Rock of

60

which you have probably heard during the past few days. Evidently he needed to assure himself afresh of his power; and it is, I believe, from the Rock that all his power on this side of the river is derived. What assurance he gained from it I do not know: what matters it? The whole life of the village has continued just as it was on the night when he grieved over its rebellion. The task of raising it to a higher spiritual and intellectual level is left to us, while he fumbles in the darkness and impotence of superstition and vents his petty malice even upon the church.'

Chapter Six

BEALE'S mood had now kindled, the flame within him fully released, so that the vicar was gripped and stifled by the fierce, inhuman vitality that burned in such strange detachment from the conflagration which raged outside, down in the fold of the clay-dumps. Though Beale's glance strayed occasionally through the window, he had obviously ceased to regard the blazing engine-house as a personal disaster that need cause him further worry. He was becoming absorbed in his mono-maniac obsession, and Mr Reed was aware that this actually did dwarf to insignificance the sharp, crude drama which had broken so unexpectedly upon the village. He was drawn towards Beale's perspective, his normal faculties dulled in the fading out of common-place interests.

'Such,' Beale resumed more quietly, 'was Potter's vision on that summer night of seventeen years ago. Why he had come to Carn Veor remains a mystery to me. I have heard that before returning back across the river he called at a house in this district and blessed a girl who had been born that day. It was a habit of his, before he found most doors closed against him, to call at cottage homes on the night of a birth and to bless the infant with a ritual which was certainly not that of any official Church.'

'Bronwen Cundy on this occasion, no doubt?' suggested Mr Reed.

'I wish I knew. But some of Potter's most dangerous moves are so shrouded in secrecy that I cannot be sure which individuals are concerned until I see the results.

It would seem that the few whom he marks in this peculiar way become useless to me; some of them go mad; and, as I have pointed out, I do not always recognize them until they have grown up and caused me to waste much effort in trying to retain them as decent reasonable citizens. After Bronwen Cundy ran off to seek Potter's protection last year I was naturally suspicious. I asked her father whether there was any unusual circumstances connected with the birth. He assured me that Potter had not entered the house — that neither his wife nor himself had ever seen Potter or had any communication with him.'

'That evidence seems conclusive,' remarked Mr Reed, smiling faintly.

'Not altogether. Cundy was at work at the time of the birth, and both his wife and the doctor are now dead, so that I am left guessing as to whether Bronwen was, in fact, the victim Potter chose that night. But I am glad to say that Mr Cundy's hostility to Potter is now typical of most parents in Carn Veor. Potter would find almost every door barred against him during a confinement: he can no longer usurp, by his quackery, the proper rites ordained and ministered by the Church to these infants. I shall watch Bronwen Cundy's development with some anxiety — I fear that in any case there is little hope of her becoming a member of the Church of England. But the general position is not a depressing one. On a very broad front Potter's influence has been broken, his pretensions exposed, and now that he no longer dares to show himself in Carn Veor, we have all this material, this younger generation, to mould for the new age, the new religious and moral sanity.'

Beale paused: he rose and stepped again to the window. For several minutes he contemplated the scene at the engine-house. The flames still fanned up from the

63

remaining beams of the roof, despite the continuous stream of water that was being pumped into the building. The smoke had become so thick that it looked like a solid pillar heaving out of the walls — a bulbous black pillar moving slowly against the white glittering sand and the pale blue sky. Beale evidently felt the spectacle as vaguely ominous, but he was not long distracted by it from the urgent personal affairs he was discussing with Mr Reed. He seemed to be using the fire as a goad to force him back with a grimmer determination upon his war with Potter. There was an ugly shadow on his face as he turned afresh to the vicar, lurched up to him and laid a hand on his shoulder.

'How, my friend, can we help to develop in these young people a balanced system of life, conditioned by a progressive Church, while at the same time leaving them free to exercise their natural desires in a normal, healthy way? That is the problem.'

'It is,' Mr Reed assented in a strained voice. The sense of unreality and fantasy was tautening upon him as his mind tussled with the two incongruous factors that confronted him — the material destruction in the background, the alien spiritual mood of the master here in the office. Beale seemed to have no difficulty in concentrating upon an abstract conflict, while for the vicar this conflict was intangible, a vast overshadowing cloud from which he instinctively sought relief in the vivid actuality of the drama down by the clay-pit. He knew that nothing he could say would be more than a perfunctory and fumbling response to Beale's thought. His initiative and power of independent judgment were drained out, stagnating in remote depths.

'These people,' Reed went on mechanically, 'regard the Christian Church as in some way connected with Potter. I find that to be the chief trouble. And it isn't easy to refute them, since I understand Potter's book was once placed on the altar during weddings in the local churches.'

'Yes, I fear such profanity did occasionally occur,' admitted Beale with an ironic twist of his eyebrows; he seemed to enjoy the distressed, bewildered glance which the vicar cast up at him through his thick lenses. 'At that time Potter tried to gain the allegiance of our young folk by setting himself up as a patron of marriage. It was, of course, merely another attempt to get the clay-lands back under his control. He hedged his patronage about with the most fantastic rules.'

'I am not surprised,' Mr Reed murmured.

'Some twenty years ago,' Beale went on, 'he endeavoured to bring in a by-law that no marriage in Carn Veor should be considered legal unless the parties had first been to his sacred Rock and observed certain rites in the primitive chapel — little more than a cave — which then stood at the end of Potter's Lane. This by-law was defeated by Ashford's predecessor, Parson Bully, and the affair closed in an incident that revealed Potter's character at its worst.'

'Indeed!' The vicar shifted uneasily, his fingers groping and twitching on the table as he looked past Beale's pacing figure at the flame-streaked cloud of smoke that shuddered and loosened under the hose-jets spraying through the windows of the engine-house. He heard the drone of the fire-engine, the dull thud of falling debris, threatening but not breaking the spell of Beale's words.

'Mr Bully was naturally curious to find why Potter was so preoccupied with his magical Rock,' resumed Beale, looming again close to the table. 'But he didn't care to enter the lane to view it near at hand, and there was no other means of access to it, as the adjoining fields

65

are bordered by marshes. Bully was an athlete, and one summer night he climbed a sycamore tree behind the chapel. From this tree he glimpsed the Rock towering weirdly above the thorns; he studied it for some time through binoculars. The next day he found that the sycamore tree had been felled — it lay prone across the road, and had crashed through the roof of the chapel. Thus in venting his spleen on Mr Bully, Potter had destroyed his own sanctuary. The place is still in ruins.'

'Why hasn't he repaired it?' asked Mr Reed vaguely.

'He probably lacks the labour and material. The whole valley is in an appalling state of neglect: Potter's Lane is like a jungle. If the land were my property I should certainly do something about it. But I have no control over the part of the valley which contains the Rock and the derelict chapel. I can only use my influence to modernize the churches here in the north: Potter clings very tenaciously to his lane, though he has not pruned a bush or cut down a nettle in it since the Rock was placed there. The lane would be of little use to me even if by a stroke of fortune it fell into my hands. It is so narrow that one could not even get a steam-roller through it. The only thing I could do would be to take some of my biggest claywork excavators down there and simply scoop up the whole mess, level the hedges and use the site for — possibly a golf course where tired businessmen from Tredoggett could come for recreation on Sundays.'

Mr Reed nodded thoughtfully.

'That would certainly be an improvement,' he remarked. 'From what I have heard it would seem that Potter's Lane is the source of all the superstition in the district. People who visit it are inclined to get — well, a little hysterical.'

Beale smiled, watching the vicar with smouldering malice.

'I fancied you would have found some evidence of that. It's odd that another instance of this lunacy should occur on the very day you were installed here. But it may be as well for you to realize what you are up against while that lane remains in Potter's hands. Apart from that he is quite definitely a spent force, discredited, ignored and largely forgotten. And because of all this you will, I think, agree that my plans for the future of Carn Veor are the only reasonable ones. We must pursue a programme of education that will give human nature its opportunity, and clear away the poison of defeatism that is bred by false and irrelevant ideas.'

'Yes, certainly,' murmured Mr Reed in a cold remote tone. He was still gazing at the fire, still trying to realize the magnitude of the whole situation that was opening round him. He felt dwarfed and submerged under the enigma of Beale.

'I always look out for the best in my fellow men,' he said, aware that he was speaking from a blunted mind, almost childishly. 'And I believe that even in these Cornish villagers there are qualities that would not continue to be anti-social if they were placed under proper guidance and brought into touch with — er — a more civilized and spiritual ethic. I assure you that I have no sympathy whatever with the offensive doctrines which seem to be generated in Potter's Lane as far as this district is concerned.' Mr Reed moistened his lips and roused, flicked into an abrupt bitterness by the abnormal pressure.

'I have, of course, encountered these retrogressive ideas elsewhere — in Essex and even at college. They have infested current theology in spite of the most strenuous efforts to keep the roads clear for the advance of rational and liberal religious thought.'

'You modernist clergy have my sympathy on that point,' responded Beale drily, his squat face puckered with sardonic relish as he leaned over the table. 'But we must concentrate upon the local aspect of this war of ideas. These villagers know nothing of what has happened to European theology during the past thirty years. They are disturbed only by the feud between myself and Potter — the antagonism between the clay-works and Potter's Lane, if you care to put it that way.'

'Everything seems to be rather crude and material-istic here,' observed Mr Reed, flushing slightly under Beale's taunt.

'Yes; we are a practical community. But with so many object lessons at the outset of your ministry in the parish, you will soon adapt yourself and make your own contribution towards the removal of this crudity on both the material and spiritual levels. I will let you know from time to time of any ventures I think it worth while to make in the village. Mr Ashford and I were consider-ing the inauguration of a psychiatric clinic just before he died, which might help neurotics to get more benefit from Adult School lectures on current scientific and political matters. Our schoolmaster, Mr Teague, would be very willing to co-operate in such activities. His more brilliant pupils complete their education outside Corn-wall and rarely return here, but those who remain must be protected against Potter's propaganda.'

'I can promise you my whole-hearted support,' said Mr Reed, still speaking unnaturally, strained and dis-torted mentally by the unknown and vaguely sinister tides that pulled upon him both from the visible world of Beale and from the hidden brooding regions of Potter's Lane. The details of the office had not for a moment

68

emerged in prosaic clarity; the room had become a vortex in which he was caught helplessly, sucked down and crushed.

Beale stepped to the door, and with his hand on the knob he turned — an ungainly but dynamic figure.

'At present,' he said, 'you can help our cause best by carrying on your routine work at the church — by assuring your parishioners that I am their friend and that the malicious attacks made against me — the clay-work fire, for instance — are completely unjustified. Do all you can also to suggest that Potter is a senile humbug, and that Mrs Yelland has been grossly deceived in supposing that Potter's Lane is a fit place for educating the religious instinct. If you can convince the woman herself of her folly, so much the better — though there is probably little hope of your doing so. Your chief concern should be to safeguard the younger generation . . . I thank you, Mr Reed.'

Beale extended his hand as the vicar rose, and a minute later Mr Reed had left the office, moving dazedly into air that reeked of oil fumes and the smell of hot, soot-blackened stone and burning wood.

Part Two

The Invasion

Between the desire
And the spasm
Between the potency
And the existence
Between the essence
And the descent
Falls the Shadow
     For Thine is the Kingdom

T. S. Eliot

Chapter Seven

ROSA NANCE, who lived in the one thatched-roofed cottage of Carn Veor, was the only person in the village who had entered Potter's Lane as a child. She had, in fact, been seduced there when she was twelve — seduced by Beale, who had waylaid her at one of the outer bends, knowing that she had gone into the lane through carnal curiosity with no thought of seeing the Rock.

Rosa had felt strange intimations of renewal in Potter's Lane before Beale intruded, as if the moods suggested and veiled by its peculiar gloom were reversals of all the values she had known in Carn Veor. She had always been different from the other village girls — intense and lonely, with a hint of the sensuous mystic about her. There in the lane she first recognized the standards and aspirations of normal life were not sufficient for her, not adequate to hold the storm of her blood, to liberate and transmute her carnal tide. Every aspect of the clay world seemed unreal in this valley, except the vague memories of baptism and burial which pierced her when she glimpsed the full, wind-shaken marshes behind the lane. The fancied virtue and supremacy of the spirit faded and dissolved for her at the touch of the shade of the thorn trees upon her bare limbs. But for Beale she would have passed through this death, she would have been reborn at the Rock, the child-self aware and baptized. But she did not even know that progress along this lane led to the Rock. And Beale had brought her the gross, unbaptized awareness of her sex, clouding her desire with a foul, murky aversion. Yet the desire remained, imprisoned within the darkness of Beale but struggling to escape into its natural use. She was soon ripe for her open downfall.

When she was fourteen a stranger, Donald Smithers, came to lodge for a few weeks with Miss Pascoe, the Carn Veor school caretaker, who lived in a house adjoining the Nances'. He was in the early thirties — a good-looking flashy town product whose genteel manners and elegant clothes aroused the awe and envy of the villagers. He noted with casual piquancy the possibilities of the Nances' daughter, who was by now grown to be a desirable and wayward girl with long golden hair crisping about her shoulders and firm, sharp breasts which had already, at her playful invitation, been fondled by several village men. She knew well enough what these male creatures wanted of her, and her experience in Potter's Lane had made her doubtful whether there were any other fulfilment than the brief carnal flame, the fulfilment beyond the hands of Beale, the new, human beginning. And so, one evening while the interest of Carn Veor was diverted — for the Nances had killed a pig and the neighbours could think of nothing but the likelihood of their receiving samples of pork and liver which would lighten their butchers' bills — Rosa and Smithers climbed stealthily to the top of one of the clay-dumps; and though the sandy bed was a little hard, it was cleaner and more delectable to Rosa than the ferns and grass of the hedgeside amid which Beale had thrown her. She felt the experience as an initiation into the new freedom, and looked to Smithers to plunge her whole nature again and again into this ecstacy until she had lost the stain of Beale's hands and was fit to marry.

But it seemed that a malicious Providence had chosen

74

Rosa for its sport. It may even have been at Potter's instigation that Smithers had come to Carn Veor. At all events, within a week of Rosa's willing surrender to him he had left the village in custody, and the last she heard of him was that he had been imprisoned for embezzling money in a Plymouth bank.

Rosa was left derelict, torn for a while by a perverse craving to return to Potter's Lane, to get beyond the point where Beale had captured her, to wring in sensual agony the uttermost secrets from the forbidden, unknown reaches of the lane. But the more natural inclination prevailed: she merely became a village prostitute, the harlot of the clayworks, haunting the pits during the night shifts and offering her services to any of the workmen who, for a few shillings, cared to enjoy her on the bare darkened sand, in the corrugated-iron cuddies, or on piles of tarpaulin in the drying-sheds and engine-houses. Beale was aware of this and approved of it, but he did not seek any further contact with her: personally he shunned her. His work was done as far as Rosa was concerned.

None of her customers guessed why she was so reluctant to lead them into the fields and soft grassy lanes, as other girls of her type were wont to do. They did not know that the magnetism of Potter's Lane was still upon her, wounding and embittering all the founts of her natural mastery. But she knew — knew that she could not always endure or resist it. The lane would win in the end, it would draw her back: her surrender was decreed. She was sure that if she returned to the lane she would not find Beale there a second time; yet, being what she was, she feared even more to meet Potter. But now, suddenly, there had come to her a hint of release from the intolerable duality, the terrifying simplicity of choosing between the two absolutes. She had heard of

something in the lane that was neither Beale nor Potter
— a mysterious image that thrilled her with furtive
imaginings of the bodily heaven unashamed, the baptism she had missed in her first pressure and unfolding
towards the flesh. The image was irrational, it seemed
crude and unspiritual, yet was strangely authentic.
Rosa was fascinated, she wished to hear more. She had
decided to enquire of Mrs Yelland exactly what it was
that she had seen in Potter's Lane last Sunday, and why
anything so commonplace should have the peculiar
effect of revitalizing the Yelland's marriage and stirring
the passions of the neighbours to heated controversy.
She supposed it would be difficult to get the facts from
Mrs Yelland, who, being virtuous, had long ceased to
be on speaking terms with Rosa. But if she was now so
radically changed, perhaps she would be friendly
enough to answer a few civil questions.

The Nance's home stood a little apart from the other
houses, continuing the row in which the Gools lived.
Between it and them was the old village pump. The
cottage faced the tiny churchyard, and was set on higher
ground than any other in Carn Veor, being the most
northerly house on the upward slope of the moor.
Northward from here the road wound on, hedgeless to
the clayworks. From the front windows of the dwelling
one could see the church tower and a corner of the sand-
dump curving round the adjacent pit-head: from the
rear one looked down past the back gardens of many
cottages to the jutting ends of the dance-hall and the
vicarage and the Gummas' home on the St Petroc
road.

Rosa left her home just before three o'clock on
Saturday afternoon, meaning to stroll through the village and, if possible, encounter Mrs Yelland. The sun's
heat, labouring down through a gusty wind, was scarcely

76

felt on Rosa's face now, and she kept her hands in the pockets of her green coat, as if in her present mood she recoiled from exposure to the confused mingling of spring sunshine and wintry air. She wanted to get past both, past all seasonal rhythms with their subtle treacheries: she wished to learn from Mrs Yelland of an unchangeable mood, a beauty untouched by the earth.

Rosa halted for a minute by her gateway, glancing up and down the road — a superb smouldering figure, bearing the rough village stamp even though her features were delicate, the skin fair, slightly freckled. Her long hair — still retaining its golden lustre in the sunshine — though in a duller light it appeared to have darkened a little since her childhood — tossed freely about her head and shoulders. She saw no one who was of much interest to her, only a staid married man — Mr Gool — staggering towards the rubbish-heap in a nearby hollow of the downs. He was leaning backwards and walking on his heels, carrying a large zinc bath from which feathers were being blown, to his evident concern. He would glance in alarm after these departing features, and quicken his pace, almost running, eager to deposit his load, which included ashes, on the heap before any more of it escaped.

Rosa strolled down towards the Square, humming a tune, though her blue eyes were sober, drawn instinctively and guiltily eastward to Carn Veor claywork. Behind the white gravel cone faint wisps of smoke were still pulsing raggedly up from the gutted engine-house, buffeted by the wind until they merged with the layer of black oily fumes that had thinned but was not yet completely dispersed. A smell of hot charred wood and brick could be distinguished when the wind blew in a level gust from the ruins. These sensory impressions distracted and fascinated Rosa; there was something uncanny in such external signs of arson while her memory was a blank, giving her no clue as in previous cases of this sort. The strangeness of this lack of personal connection bred in her a sense of unreality, fantasy, as if she were in some new region of uncontrolled, spontaneous outbreaks of destruction on which her own will and actions had no effect. She felt loosened, confused, and the feeling drove her back even more insistently upon the hint of a secure, dependable world of which Mrs Yelland had been speaking.

The village was more brisk now, and three cars bearing claywork officials from the engine-house passed her before she had drawn level with the Gools' home. The door was shut, but all the others in the row were open, and in several of the doorways men were lounging, children sitting or playing, or women standing, engaged in gossip with neighbours across the street. There was much animated discussion of the claywork fire, and many eyes turned with baffled suspicion on Rosa as she sauntered by, almost in the centre of the road. The eyes of the women in particular were hostile, smouldering with latent jealousy. Each of them instinctively rejected the idea that Rosa was innocent on this occasion; each of the married women harboured a dark goading fear that her husband had recently lain with Rosa in the engine-house, and that the little culprit had lied in blaming the affair on the departed Balker.

Rosa passed around the corner in silence, without being greeted by anyone, and on entering the Square she found herself in more agreeable company. In turning the bend she almost collided with Bert Truscott on his bicycle, and the shock halted her back to the course of habit, the impudent teasing of the male appetite.

Bert had possessed a unique lure for her during recent years — the lure of the fighting animal. His big fists, his scarred face with the clumsy, battered nose and ears, pulled upon her desire with a rough flavour of violence that was particularly congruous to her. She attended most of his fights, and as she saw the blood stream down his cheeks, his mouth harden with pain, his eyes gleam dangerously, she would drift into a drowsy sensual twilight of tension and conflict, more gratifying to the perverse side of her nature than mere caresses. She knew that he had just been to Tredoggett to see the promotor of his next boxing match, and the fact gave a piquant grossness to her greeting.

'Hello, Bertie! How's your sparring-partner?'

He grinned slyly back at her over his shoulder.

'Which sort? That's the point. If you mean the fluffy one at Beale's . . . I shall find out when I see her tonight.'

'Oh! I thought you'd be barging in there,' commented Rosa with scorn. 'But it might be better to wait a day or two. Beale won't be in the best temper this evening now he's had another flare up on his clayworks. Have you heard about it?'

'Saw the smoke as I was coming up the valley,' Bert replied. He braked hard, set one foot on the road and turned round on his seat. ' "Ah! There's one more hot place for Beale," I says to myself. "Rosa been busy again!" '

'Well, you were wrong this time. It wasn't anything to do with me.'

'Expect me to believe that?' Bert chuckled.

'It's true. You'll hear it around the village. I haven't been there for weeks . . . In fact, you're the last fellow I had, Wednesday night in the lodge. So it's nothing for you to be jealous about.'

79

As he realized that she was not joking, Bert looked disappointed, puzzled.

'Accident was it?'

'No. It seems Ed Balker gave sixpence to Tucker's little boy — you know the brother of the servant there at Beale's — and told him to creep in the engine-house today and put a match to the oil drum. They've caught the boy and he's owned up. So this is Ed's parting shot — no blame on me whatever.'

'You and Ed haven't been together in that engine-house?'

'No. Nor anywhere else. You know his name hasn't been coupled with mine!' Rosa spoke with a sudden vehemence that surprised Bert, and revealed something of its cause as she added with an abrupt change of tone, her eyes averted:

'He's too close to Beale — that's why. I had to keep clear.'

'Well, I'm damned!' exclaimed Bert, uncomprehending — for he, like all the villagers, was ignorant of Rosa's seduction as a child in Potter's Lane. 'This is a queer business. First fire on the clayworks for the past ten years that wasn't somehow mixed up wi' your little games! I should think there was meaning in it.'

'What meaning?'

'Come to a turning point in our history here to Carn Veor — something like that,' replied Bert. 'What with Ed clearing out and Mrs Yelland finding Potter's Rock — and now this smoke in the sky that isn't Rosa's for once — things is on the move. And there may be other funny moves soon.'

'About you and Florrie?'

'I didn't mean that. I was thinking of Joe Gool. Passed him just now down Tredoggett way. Looking like a chap lost and stolen he was. Bronwen give'n the slip, most likely, wi' some Tredoggett bloke. He'd be glad o' some help tonight if you'm so jealous about me going out to Florrie's.'

'Pooh! Joe!' said Rosa derisively, and as Bert cycled on around the corner — he lived just opposite the Gools' — she glanced towards Bronwen's home.

As she watched the door opened and Timothy strode out, carrying a pitcher. He turned in her direction, heading for the pump. He was stripped to his shirt for a wash, but had found that no clean water was available indoors; and walking in his usual erect and dignified manner he suggested a virility as potent as Bert's, with the added fascination of being to Rosa a detached, unconquered territory — for he had so far remained indifferent to her solicitations.

Rosa decided to enquire at once whether Bert's hint was true.

'Is Bronwen in?' she asked halting directly in Timothy's path.

'She isn't, to the moment,' replied Timothy in a weighty tone. He jerked his hand towards the lower end of the street. 'Gone to shop for lard — and must ha' stopped talking wi' somebody — been gone ten minutes.' He spat, walking round Rosa with a solemn and judicious shake of the head. 'Plenty for the women to chatter about this week-end.'

'Yes, things are warming up,' agreed Rosa, sobering as she passed on.

Her thoughts had reverted to her personal quest, and on reaching the grocery store in the main street she was startled by a sense that her movements had been guided.

Inside the shop three persons were listening with slightly bored expressions to a stream of words from a

81

rough, emphatic voice. These three were Mrs Budge, the shop-keeper, Maggie Gumma and Bronwen; and the speaker was Mrs Yelland.

Chapter Eight

BUDGE'S grocery store was a poky little place, rarely sunlit because of its small window, dimly lighted in the winter evenings by an oil lamp that hung above the counter. Large tins were piled along the walls below shelves which displayed a colourful assortment of packets and jars. The counter was short, and on one end of it stood a pair of scales, several loaves of bread, and a chunk of lard covered with tissue paper.

When Mrs Yelland entered the shop Mrs Budge was leaning over the desk behind the counter, on the right hand side of the doorway. She held a pencil and was totalling an account. She glanced up as Mrs Yelland stepped briskly over the threshold, and her face expressed chagrin. Mrs Budge was a woman in her early forties, large-boned and masculine in appearance. Her chin and upper lip showed a dark growth of hair, which she clipped with her scissors every Sunday morning before going to church. Her eyebrows were exceptionally thick, shooting towards the main mass of her hair, that was jet black and frizzy. Her limbs were muscular and her voice rumbled as deeply as a man's. She was the mother of five children.

Mrs Yelland, neatly garbed now in a grey coat and black straw hat, moved up to the counter and placed a sixpence with a clatter on the scratched board.

'Packet o' peas, Mrs Budge.'

Mrs Budge sniffed, dropped her pencil and lurched around the corner of the desk. She turned to take a green packet from one of the shelves and remarked casually:

'Yelland's gone over engine-house to see the fire, I suppose?'

'He strolled over for a minute, but didn't stop when he found 'twas only a little boy's doings,' Mrs Yelland replied. 'He's a quiet fellow — would rather be in practising with his draughts board than looking at a fire brigade unless it minded him of Rosa. Always was mad about draughts ever since I knew him. He's home there now with his board, clicking the men around; aiming to win the next championship over to pub.'

'And leaving you to tackle the garden, as usual?'

'Yes — as usual,' declared Mrs Yelland gleefully as she received the peas. 'I've turned in three rows since dinner-time and I'm enjoying it this year, for the first time in me life.'

Mrs Budge tossed the coin into the till, frowning in silence over the scales in a way that decidedly repelled any further advance in the conversation.

Mrs Yelland accepted the challenge. She seated herself on a high chair just opposite the shop-keeper, and grinning in the shadow of the lard she resumed aggressively:

'Things was going from bad to worse between me and Yelland. I was at me wits' end and begun spring-cleaning jist to work off me feelings and to take me mind off the squabbles. 'Twas early — too early wi' the gardening and all; but I aren't regretting it. You know why, Mrs Budge?'

'I've heard,' said Mrs Budge gruffly.

'Yes; everybody in the village have — I've took good care o' that.' Mrs Yelland chuckled. 'In turning out the old trunk upstairs I came across Potter's book, and dipped into it as I sat back on the bed to rest for a few minutes. Years since I'd read it and I'd nigh forgot what 'twas about. 'Tis a guide-book to our district, and I

84

found Potter'd mentioned a holy Rock in the middle of his lane where a lot o' folks had been cured o' their ailments in bygone times. I minded hearing about and thought I'd go along and see if 'twas still there. "Can't do no harm," I says to meself. "Maybe I shall come back same as I went, but it couldn't make things worser." And as it happened . . . well, you know how everybody's talking. 'Tis a fair miracle, the difference in our home this last week. Not a cross word between me and Yelland since Sunday.'

Mrs Budge was glaring through the window, and she spoke over her shoulder, superciliously.

'Didn't Ellen Pascoe, the school caretaker, go to Potter's Lane the same night you went?'

'I've heard she did,' came Mrs Yelland's grudging reply, 'but I doubt it meself.'

'She was seen going in lane,' persisted Mrs Budge. 'And Mrs Prynne saw her passing Gummas' on her way home, stumbling along in the gutter and crying her heart out. So if she did see the Rock it only brought misery to her. I saw her Tuesday morning — she came in here for starch — and her face was like a fiddle. Hardly spoke a word, either. 'Twasn't like Ellen Pascoe at all. How d'you account for that?'

'There's a fault somewhere,' admitted Mrs Yelland, apparently addressing a bowl of bananas set on a packing case just inside the doorway. 'But — if she did go through the lane — 'tisn't in Potter; 'tis in Miss Pascoe.'

'Do you know anything against her?'

'None of us can judge. Maybe there's a guilty secret she got what she ha'n't spoke of: that would keep her shut up . . .'

Mrs Yelland paused: footsteps were heard approaching from the street. At the next moment Bronwen tripped into the store, followed by Maggie Gumma — a big slatternly creature in her early thirties, obviously near her time. Maggie carried an oil can.

Mrs Budge's relief was undisguised. She moved to the end of the counter furthest from Mrs Yelland, suggesting by her attitude that no one but herself had hitherto been present. Mrs Yelland rose and, leaning back against the counter, grinned at the two newcomers, hinting that her presence should be a pleasant surprise to them.

'So you want oil, Maggie?' remarked Mrs Budge, twisting her lips in something that might, with a little more effort, have become a smile. 'In a minute. I'll tend Bronwen first if you don't mind. Sit down on chair while you'm waiting. You need to rest a bit before you go back. Should think your mother could ha' come now 'tis so close.'

Maggie looked suspiciously at the chair, evidently doubting whether it would bear her weight.

'No, mother couldn't — her corns is took bad,' said Maggie, mumbling the words. 'She's sitting in doorway with her shoes off: corns begun pricking all of a sudden, just after Mrs Gool left us.'

'I seen Mrs Gool go past, carrying a fowl,' observed Mrs Yelland, casting a sharp glance at Bronwen. 'Getting ready for the visitors tomorrow, I s'pose?'

As Maggie heavily seated herself the shop-keeper leaned towards Bronwen, who had ignored Mrs Yelland's remark.

'And what do *you* want, Bronwen?'

'Lard, please — half a pound,' said Bronwen nervously. 'I've run short of it — and in the midst of baking. I thought to have had pasties ready for tea, but 'twill be a late one, I'm afraid.' She stepped close up behind Mrs Yelland, opening her purse.

Mrs Yelland tapped her shoulder with the packet of peas.

'I spied Joe going to Potter's, Bronwen.'

The girl's face clouded, though her lips twitched into an uneasy smile.

'Oh — yes, I daresay. He's on his way back by now. We shall be very grateful to you if — if he's lucky: he wouldn't have tried this opening if it hadn't been for you.'

Mrs Yelland replied so sternly that all three of her hearers stared at her in astonishment.

'I've talked o' more things than Potter wanting chaps to work for'n,' she said, her eyes fixed piercingly on Bronwen's face. 'I hope Joe'll get his job, but I can't promise. I'd have felt easier if he'd been with 'ee down to Potter's Lane. I told 'ee so this morning.'

Bronwen made an impatient gesture, watching Mrs Budge slice the lard.

'I don't see that got anything to do with it,' she stated. 'If Joe's fit for the work . . .'

'Maybe he isn't fit.'

'But he's a lot stronger: he looks so and feels so.'

'Potter got his own standards o' fitness,' Mrs Yelland answered quietly, 'and p'raps they demand something more than strong limbs.'

Bronwen flushed, handing a shilling to Mrs Budge while looking askance at Maggie, who held the oil can on her lap, hands clasped over its mouth, her chin resting on a flabby wrist. She was gazing stonily at the floor, taking no interest in the discussion.

Bronwen turned spiritedly to Mrs Yelland.

'Well, if 'tis good character a chap got to have,' she retorted, 'Joe's safe enough. You all know that. He's never touched a girl till I took up with him.'

Mrs Yelland and Mrs Budge peered at Bronwen dubiously. They had not forgotten the indoor phase of Joe's courtship, the periods when his kindly and trustful parents had sat downstairs, perhaps discreetly listening to the radio as they waited for Bronwen to leave the bedroom.

'Well, I admit,' said Mrs Yelland after a rather lengthy pause, 'we don't know anything agin Joe: I wouldn't scandal the man. But Potter knows more secret things than do meet our eyes. Maybe 'tis things that ha'n't been done, and not things that have, what'll knock Joe out.'

'Oh, you're a wet blanket!' exclaimed Bronwen irritably.

Mrs Budge, wrapping the slice of lard, nodded derisively at Mrs Yelland.

'She can't think o' nothing apart from Potter, Bronwen. She been telling about'n again. He've done her a world o' good, it seems, and made her enjoy shovelling potatoes.'

'And so he have,' broke in Mrs Yelland, unruffled and quick to seize the opportunity of resuming her recital. 'Other years I've hated it — you don't need me to tell 'ee — hated it and near hated the poor fellow who left me to do sich work: and 'twould have been the same this year if . . .'

Noting that Bronwen had glanced swiftly towards the street through the open doorway, Mrs Yelland paused. Other footsteps were heard, and a minute later the threshold was shadowed as Rosa ascended the step, her green coat now unfastened, showing the red jumper and grey skirt beneath.

'So 'tis you this time, Miss Nance?' the shop-keeper greeted, looking at Rosa with a sour curiosity, her thoughts jolted by reminders of the claywork fire.

'Yes — but I aren't come to buy anything,' responded Rosa, lounging against the jamb and tossing back her hair. 'I've just been looking for Mrs Yelland.'

Mrs Yelland's eyes went very wide open.

'Looking for me?'

'Yes. I — I've heard so much, it's natural . . . They're all talking about you — on the clayworks — everywhere. And I want to know . . .' She paused, and it was noticed that she breathed heavily, though she had not hurried to the shop. 'You guess, I daresay, what I want to hear about.'

Mrs Yelland glanced wistfully around the store; she was tired and wished that another chair was handy. Nothing resembling a seat was available, however, except an inverted lard box in the corner behind the bananas, and she couldn't very well sit on that.

While she hesitated Mrs Budge leaned over the counter, tapping Maggie's arm.

'Your can, Maggie.'

The woman gave a start, blinking foolishly up into Mrs Budge's face, then clumsily handed her the oil can and a few pence taken from a pocket of her apron.

Bronwen and Rosa watched Mrs Budge leave the shop and move with long strides past the window towards the coal-shed, where the oil tank was kept.

Mrs Yelland stepped abruptly forward and caught Rosa's sleeve, directing her attention exclusively to Rosa, who was likely to prove her most attentive listener. She spoke close to the girl's ear, though loudly.

'I been telling o' the squabbles me and Yelland used to have over the gardening,' she began. 'Sometimes when I came in wi' me back aching and feeling fair done up — for I had me housework to do besides — Yelland would be sitting quiet by the fire over his draughts board, and I'd let rip. "You lazy lout!" I'd shout at'n.

89

"I'm darned if I'll get any supper for 'ee." He'd just go on clicking the men around the board, whistling a tune to aggravate me and going very red and sulky in the face. I'd flounce around getting me own supper down other end o' the table, and then stump off to roost by meself. I'd hear him rattling dishes and upsetting things as he poured his tea and cut a few slices o' bread and cake, then he'd come creeping upstairs, grunting in the dark, while I nagged and fumed on me pillow. That was our married life.'

'Well,' Bronwen challenged, tucking the lard under her arm, 'what difference has it made, seeing this Rock o' Potter's?'

'You can see for yourself,' replied Mrs Yelland, nodding an acknowledgment across at Bronwen while she still addressed Rosa. 'I've turned in five rows today, and I aren't complaining: me garden do look better teeled than most men's in the village. Yelland's home playing draughts with hisself and wondering what he've done to deserve sich a good wife: those was his own words last night as we was undressing. I believe I'll get him to go along too yet; but I aren't waiting till then before I try to get the place moving. There's plenty o' folks here wi' troubles worse than mine was.'

Rosa was deeply impressed, for though this testimony came from a more practical and prosaic level than that on which she lived, it confirmed her instinctive knowledge that Potter's Lane was the source of the power she needed. She gazed out into the street, her lip bitten; and though PC Rodda passed by at that moment, grinning across at her — for she had sometimes solaced him during night vigils when he was investigating a larceny on the clayworks — she made no response. She was beyond that, already beyond it, in a sort of void.

Mrs Yelland, who stood with Rosa in the doorway,

turned to notice the effect of her words on Maggie and Bronwen. These two were staring at each other dully, peevishly. A frown wrinkled Bronwen's forehead, her lips were drawn up in a pout. She was worrying about Joe . . . But Mrs Yelland could waste no more advice on that problem. She stepped back to Maggie and laid a hand sympathetically on her shoulder.

'You got a big enough trouble, chiel, everybody can tell. And I've been hearing things besides,' she added darkly.

To the surprise of her friends Maggie began sobbing.

'Yes,' she blurted from behind her hands; 'I — I ha'n't been meself at all this past week. Me and George — falled out last Sunday: first time for months — and I'd thought things were getting better. And now of all times . . . I'm afraid what's going to happen. 'Twas all over nothing — mother's fault more than ours; but he ha'n't kissed me since. He wouldn't sleep wi' me if there was room anywhere else, and as 'tis he only swear at me and threaten to push me out o' bed if I don't lie quiet.'

'There you be!' cried Mrs Yelland, shaking her fist at Mrs Budge, who returned at that moment with the filled oil can. 'Love is sweet enough when it d'come first to you Carn Veor maids, but it soon get a different taste wi' Beale's influence creeping in — the men working for'n in the open on his clayworks, and the women serving him mostly without knowing it, like I did.'

As Mrs Budge dropped the oil can by the counter, Rosa turned her back to the group. She did not wish them to glimpse the emotions, bitter, stark and hungry, that her face expressed. She clasped her hands. And the sights and sounds of Potter's Lane flowed in upon her consciousness in a wave that shook aside the torpor of selfhood. Not the self now, not even the body within

91

nature, but the death, the renewal beyond the self. It awaited her in the lane. She again saw herself hurrying under the thorn trees, startling the birds and being in turn startled by the sense of intruders, absolute values not of Nature but of the great transmutation. She saw herself drawing near to a point in the lane where the taint of the blood was lost, shame and pride purged from the spirit, all ideals and striving after self-fulfilment renounced. There was the baptism from which her body would rise with breasts that could not be held by death, loins that could suffer no invasion from the dark betrayer, the pagan fecundity. Rosa knew now that she must press back into that experience and complete it, or die within the shade of Beale. She could not return to the natural shadow in which Smithers had left her.

Rosa glanced at Bronwen, her eyes stormy and wild with desire.

'I want to go back — I want to go!' she cried.

Mrs Yelland, who had been instructing Mrs Budge about the bananas, nodded at Rosa approvingly. She felt the anguish in the girl's voice and manner, but was not deflected by it from her cool, bustling practicality.

'You wouldn't regret it, Rosa; and 'twould be a blessing for all Carn Veor. Even Beale must feel he've lost enough engine-houses, even if this latest one isn't on your conscience. 'Tis time Beale's clayworks was cleaned up: I've heard Yelland tell what he've seen . . . Well, we all know about it. I won't say no more. But go down like I did, Rosa, and you'll find the difference.'

Bronwen laid a restraining hand on Rosa's arm.

'No, don't Rosa — don't listen! You know what we've been told about that lane. I didn't think of it last Summer, I was in such a panic; but I've been glad since that I went in the wrong lane and not Potter's. They say if you go in there something'll take your guts out and you'll be spoilt for the sort o' lanes we're used to — or for decent marriage either.'

Rosa frowned, watching Mrs Budge slip two bananas from the bowl into a paper bag and place them on the counter beside Mrs Yelland's peas.

'I have my own reasons for doubting that,' she said more calmly, almost in a whisper. 'But even if 'twas true that Potter hates that sort o' love I'd still want to go. 'Twould be a relief from — Beale's clayworks.'

'Hearken to that!' cried Mrs Yelland, pointing at Rosa while eyeing her companions triumphantly. 'There's your love what you'm so proud of and can't afford to have spoilt.'

Bronwen flushed.

'We aren't all like Rosa,' she said hotly.

Mrs Yelland fumbled in her purse for a few more pence to pay for the fruit, but while handing the money to Mrs Budge she addressed the trio behind her.

'One man or many, 'tis all the same if you let Beale have his way with it. You can get sick o' your own man as well as somebody else's . . .'

Rosa left the threshold abruptly, and having stumbled down the steps she moved blindly into the sunlit road, her face tense with decision.

As Maggie rose, dabbing at her eyes with her sleeve, Bronwen felt stifled by the deadly pressure of unhappiness about her. She read the dull despair on Maggie's flabby, tear-stained face. She glanced at the surly visage of Mrs Budge, retiring behind the counter — a visage marked by the clawing of a beast under the cloak of respectability. She felt the condition of her own heart — chilled, rather bored, restless. And along the duct of her awareness of Beale came the dim, stinging apprehension.

Mrs Yelland was right. Love, to the inhabitants of

93

Carn Veor, was a mockery. Its landscape was an evil thing — a bed of primitive slime, a bed for wallowing but not for joy. The clean, firm clay-peaks were a mirage; they were not peaks of vision, for there was no vision here — only the pillared male darkness brooding above the female swamp, sucked down in the dream-illusion of security until the swamp heaved with horrible distortions, the reptilian life of the womb. Here was the raw, unredeemed instinct of copulation and breeding, a process that left the ultimate aim unrealized, the true womb barren, the heart of male flesh unsatisfied, homeless, vulnerable. And the instinct was not intact even within its own limits. There was a stain, a corruption from within, fusing always with the shadow from without, the pagan soil that was twilight, the will of Beale that was the outer darkness into which Nature faded.

These vague impressions angered Bronwen; she stepped back, taking the lard, to the door.

'That may be so,' she admitted. 'Marriage and babies mayn't be all 'tis supposed to be; but Potter's Rock can't touch that, whatever you may think.' She nudged Maggie as the young woman slouched past her, dangling the oil can.

'Isn't it nonsense, Mag? Potter must be dotty. And now if Rosa gets caught . . .'

Bronwen's face became suddenly pale, stiffened. As her eyes took in the lower end of the street she saw Joe turn the corner by the school — a thin, bowed, weakly figure, groping his way along the ditch. She ran at once down the steps, down the street towards him, her heart swooping wild and cold. For she knew, even in her first glimpse of him, before either of them spoke that his errand had been fruitless.

'Oh, Joe!' she cried in strangling dismay. 'You — you've *failed*!'

Joe's body was wrenched to a standstill; he reeled, leaning against a gatepost and lifting to her a face she scarcely recognized. She was shocked by his changed appearance. He looked old and exhausted, but it was not simply a physical weariness due to his long journey. His look was that of a man who in blind presumption had ventured further than any mortal should go, and been drained out or burnt out by a stroke from the unknown. The jollity, and even the queer half-malicious perversity of his natural self were gone. He was sullen and bitter, and his revolt was not that of one who had been duped or ill-used by a fellow creature; it was darkly blasphemous, the writhing of a soul aroused and aware of its primal antagonist. He was at war with the Almighty as he slumped there with his hands clenched and his glowering face turned towards Bronwen.

Her sudden emergence confused him. He had thought to reveal his news in privacy, where the tide of despair could sweep them into the sensual heart of rebellion. The thwarted hunger had almost maddened him as he crossed the sandbanks on which he had walked with Bronwen and Mr Reed a few hours earlier. He had looked up at the barricade which he had strengthened so hopefully, and felt that, had Bronwen come to meet him now, he would have thrown her down upon those gravel ridges and ravished her, so completely had the purity of his love perished with the perishing of hope. But those horrors were stemmed, broken by the commonplace sight of Bronwen among the group of customers at Budge's shop. Seeing Mrs Yelland and Maggie on the steps and Mrs Budge in the doorway, watching him over their heads, Joe reacted fiercely.

'Yes — Potter won't help us,' he replied hoarsely to Bronwen's greeting. 'I only saw the servant, same as

95

Mrs Yelland there, but the bitch had a pretty different story for me! Told me Potter's particular who he gives jobs to. My name wasn't on the list of — of decent and respectable chaps, I suppose!' Joe laughed cynically, rallying and stepping out beside Bronwen.

'I know what it means,' he cried, his voice tense and shrill. 'Potter's been told about we courting indoors. Beale's right: the fellow's a dirty-minded sneak, having his spite out on we young ones.'

Maggie came heavily down to the road, shrinking afresh as she felt the movements of her child, the burden of fecundity that sharpened her irrational and superstitious fears.

'You ought to have knowed that all along,' she mumbled. 'You was a fool to go. We all know what Potter did to Arthur Geach and Nina Grose; and now he's laughing at the way he's fooled you and stopped 'ee from getting married.'

Mrs Yelland's face was grave, stern though compassionate. She addressed Bronwen.

'Neither of 'ee,' she said, 'would listen when you was going home to dinner just now, when I advised 'ee to go down to the lane. P'raps you'll mind it now and take me hint, as Rosa have done.'

Bronwen slipped an arm about Joe's waist, and as she drew him forward her eyes flashed angrily at Mrs Yelland. Something of Joe's mood had flowed into her; the face was naked and sensual, the loose locks of gingery hair licking around it like dull flames.

'Shut up!' Bronwen shouted. 'We've had enough o' your beastly Potter. What the devil's he good for? turning Joe down like this! We'll never go on our knees to such a scoundrel. He can keep his bloody Rock to himself.'

A gripped, shocking silence fell upon the street then

came the sound of a dull, rending explosion in the distance which sent a tremor through the earth into the village. It was caused by a blast in a neighbouring clay-pit, but it seemed none the less ominous in relation to Bronwen's defiant outburst. Mrs Yelland seemed apprehensive lest it should be followed by more potent signs in the heavens, and as she watched the couple move stiffly around the corner she raised both hands towards the sky.

Chapter Nine

WHEN Beale returned to the manor after the engine-house fire had been extinguished, he went straight to the study. He was ruffled and harassed, and wished to brood in the room that was least likely to be entered by Florrie or the servant. It was now clear that, following a prolonged lull, his battle with Potter was again becoming tense, heading up to a crisis. And he was distracted by personal, irrelevant setbacks, so that it was not easy for him to concentrate on the main issue.

The familiar features of the study helped him towards such concentration. He seated himself in his favourite arm-chair beside the large bay window, and looked with a certain massive appeal about his room where so many of his designs had been formed through hours of solitary thinking, sometimes discussed with influential figures in the religious life of the county. The overthrow of Potter had been planned within these walls, which held the appearance, and even the atmosphere, of darkness. They were panelled, dark brown oak, and the curtains were heavy, black chenille: all the furniture was of sombre mould and colour. A few Hogarth prints, hung on the panelling, added to the general gloom an element of the sinister and vicious.

Beale folded his arms and frowned across at the largest bookcase in the room, a ponderous oaken structure facing the window, containing several hundred volumes. Though he was too engrossed in business and public life to have much time for reading, these books had often induced a mood in which it was easy for him to believe that Potter had been finally banished from the clay-land. None of them was crudely atheistic or obscene: he derived no personal satisfaction from such works, though when he was governor of the asylum across the river he had let them circulate among the inmates. Here at the manor he fed his mind on literature that was more dangerous to everything Potter stood for. Works of idealist philosophy and scientific humanism predominated, and there were many volumes on religion written from the standpoint of natural mysticism, or reverently critical scholarship. Most of the great romantic poets and novelists were represented. But now as his thought ranged over the fields covered by these books he was oppressed by a sense of futility. They had served him well in former conflicts in the world of ideas, but they were useless against the elemental powers that Potter had now released. Potter was attacking him this time through illiterates, people who could not be influenced by any arguments or appeals based on reason and culture. And Beale could not protect these simple folk by any more gross or sensually attractive methods than those he had already used. He knew that this battle could not be fought and won on the material level.

Beale was not a materialist. He could use materialism for his own ends, but he judged the values of his own life and business by a standard darkly spiritual, almost mystical in its indifference to worldly gain or loss. He could bear material losses without complaint if they meant spiritual gain to him. His seduction of Rosa had resulted indirectly in a financial loss of several hundred pounds, for though his claywork buildings were insured the temporary stoppage or curtailment of work involved in their destruction reduced the output of clay for the markets. But he still felt that he had made a good

99

bargain, that his gain was more real and satisfying than bricks and mortar or a favourable balance-sheet for his claywork companies. He could even look gloatingly upon his blazing sheds and engine-houses while his mental eye pictured the tormented husband, the broken home, of which the conflagration was a symbol. His enjoyment was crude, almost infantile; he was not bound by the adult, mercenary standards which dominated so many of his friends and fellow-workers. Nor was he, in the modern sense, a subtle man. He could use subtlety to achieve his ultimate purpose, but that purpose was always simple and barbaric — the lust to destroy. And sometimes the mask fell from that ultimate essence. Most of the men who worked with him or under him had seen him in moments when the infernal element was revealed, straining to possess him wholly. There had been ugly rumours similar to that which ascribed to Potter the killing of two lovers by the river bank. Nothing could be proved against him, but it was generally recognized that this moving force behind the cultural uplift of the county, this philanthropist and pioneer of the civilized ideal, was a baffling enigma, himself the embodiment of dark superstition, cunning and savagery.

Beale felt that another of those primeval, anarchic moments was now approaching. There was an ominous stillness within him, a contracting towards the volcanic regions, the demonic border-line. Not because of Balker's departure or because in his petty spite he had bribed a boy to burn down an engine-house. Such acts of human malice were common enough in Beale's world, and he regarded them with sardonic detachment. But apart from and above these movements was something else, the ultimate, deadly terror. He had been touched, invaded by the Shadow which had been

100

banished from Carn Veor for many years. The shadow of a Rock.

Two women in the village, Mrs Yelland and Miss Pascoe, had done a dangerous thing last week. They had read Potter's guide-book and been reminded afresh of the hypnotic powers of the lane in the valley. There had been results, and Mrs Yelland, at least, was articulate about them. These two women were not in themselves vital to Beale's moral control, though he had fed greedily on a certain incident in Miss Pascoe's life that was now rendered insubstantial to him, covered by the Shadow. But the dark, poisoning horror might spread to other hearts, change their orbit, still their pulsations within him, integrate them with the rhythm outside, the dayspring from Potter's land. If that occurred his hunger would become a maniacal craving; the mask would fall.

Beale had made his plan to meet this contingency. He knew well enough what would happen tomorrow night if the power of the Rock robbed him, this week-end, of any major possession. He had imagined every detail just now as, emerging from the smoke-screen that veiled Carn Veor, he looked away eastward to the sharp distant cones around Helburn Pit. He could never fully expose himself on this side of the river. He would have to return to his oldest claywork and the adjoining asylum, if only for a few hours, and pass into the other shadow, the blind, alien life of an under-world.

There were reasons why Beale wished to avoid such moments of unveiling. They occurred only when he was stripped to the black entrails of despair and temporarily admitted to himself that his struggle was hopeless. His mind turned from the irrelevancies of the bookcase and swung back to his interview with Mr Reed. The vicar, at least, had become his ally, and something might yet be done, from the pulpit, to cope with the excitement produced by Mrs Yelland's discovery. This homely woman was at present the person in Carn Veor whom Beale most hated. His rage against her was almost insane. He wished her dead, and let his imagination play upon this desire, stimulating the nerve of macabre violence that would be bared tomorrow night if the vicar's efforts were unavailing.

While he was visualizing Mrs Yelland's funeral, seeing the coffin pass through the room between him and those books, he was interrupted by the unexpected entrance of Florrie. The thin wolfish figure, clad in a red jumper and white skirt, glided inside the doorway and paused, her green glittering eyes darting coldly to Beale.

'D'you want any tea, Dad?' she greeted, her voice shrill and metallic. 'I've just laid mine. Tucker's too frightened to handle a dish without breaking it.'

Beale glanced up, rather dazed for a moment as his mind hovered between the spiritual and material situations.

'What's wrong with the girl?' he asked absently.

'Terrified of what you may do to her, I suppose. It's natural.'

'Why?'

'The fire, of course. Now she knows her brother's responsible . . .'

'Oh, that!' Beale shrugged, his swarthy face relaxed, sunken between the black-coated shoulders and the white, uncovered hair. 'She needn't fear any unpleasant consequences.'

'You won't give her notice?'

'No; it's no fault of hers.'

'And the boy?'

'I shall not take any proceedings — against anyone. You know I never do after these fires.'

'But this is an exception. It isn't Rosa . . .'

'No matter. It's your rascal of a husband, so there's compensation as usual — another broken home.'

'Yes — your own home,' she said, jeering. 'You over-played yourself with Ed. It can't make you feel too confident of your power to hold people . . . But about tea: are you hungry after all this excitement?'

Beale was stung; he lurched to his feet threateningly.

'You ought to know by this time,' he muttered between his teeth, 'that when I want tea I come to the dining-room for it.'

Florrie was alert, unperturbed; she approached him with a cajoling smile.

'I saw Bronwen Cundy at Tredoggett this morning,' she observed.

'Well? Did it remind you of anything?'

'Yes,' said Florrie, watching him with guarded malice. 'Why don't you try to pull her in again? You must have meant to set her going when you chose her last year as carnival queen but you've seemed to let her drift since then.'

Beale dropped back into his chair; he shook his head and an absent look came to his eyes. He was evidently seeing Bronwen, her most secret motives and acts, passing before him as Mrs Yelland's coffin had done, present by the creative power of his will.

'I ventured a little too soon with her,' he said moodily, 'and when she ran off seeking Potter's protection there was nothing more I could do until the mood had passed.'

'Everyone seems to have forgotten now about that fête,' remarked Florrie. 'The memory must be a night-mare to the virtuous, like a glimpse of Hell: you and I going all out in our revenge on that girl. It was worthwhile to lose Bronwen to get such an outbreak — the rows and fights, and then the orgy after dark . . .'

Beale nodded reminiscently.

'Yes, there are compensations. Luckily, she went in the wrong lane and returned home to continue a neutral attitude to our struggle. She feels herself again a simple child of the earth, under neither Potter's rule nor mine. Her only vision is a dim memory of a dead horse, a poisoned well, and rats scampering under a hedge. These may mean to her the last things of Nature, the undertones of terror and mystery waiting somewhere for her beneath the merriment of her freedom. But to be gripped by Potter she must feel the sublime.'

'She's been so innocent, I thought you'd find her a nuisance,' commented Florrie.

'No. It's only those who are prepared to obey Potter — obey him to the letter, asking no questions — whom I've got to deal seriously with. Although she never goes into the claywork buildings, even with Joe Gool. . .'

'They'd find 'em rather chilly after the Gools' front room! But his family are decent, strict sort of people: it put a brake on her I expect. She'd have been a wild one if she hadn't fallen in love with that little weakling.'

'Well, as I was saying,' resumed Beale, 'though Bronwen never enters my buildings, she keeps an equal distance from anything that might bring her under Potter's influence. In a test — and I believe a test has come this very afternoon — I have no doubt that she would take my side and not that of my enemy.' He glanced up sharply as Florrie moved to the door.

'By the way, have you seen her father lately?'

Florrie at once flushed, and stepping back to the bookcase she smiled upon the volumes, as if, with herself and Timothy, they knew a dark secret.

'Oh now — I don't think you need to ask,' she replied

104

without looking at Beale. 'It hasn't leaked out and Bronwen doesn't suspect anything. But it's gone the whole hog and I've set him itching. He'll want to splice it, that's pretty certain. I've seen it coming, and — well, I may have wanted it.'

Beale nodded at the electric fire that was now cold and dark.

'Edward is gone,' he observed, 'and I feel sure Cundy will not be long in seizing his chance. He may be here tonight. I just thought you'd better be prepared. Bert Truscott has the first claim, remember.'

Florrie prodded both her hollow cheeks with the thumb and forefinger of her right hand.

'I know I took on with Bert first,' she admitted grudgingly. 'But he's been so hot after Rosa lately that I've almost given him up. I'd rather have a man who could be relied upon to some extent; and I haven't heard that Tim has played loose with any others since his wife died.'

'He hasn't,' Beale assured her. 'Cundy is a more domesticated man than Truscott ever could be, and once settled, you'd have no trouble with him.'

After a short silence Florrie turned from the bookcase, smiling wickedly.

'I've made my choice,' was her cryptic statement as, leaving Beale, she closed the door of his study.

Chapter Ten

A FEW minutes after Florrie left him Beale rose and crossed to the big arched window. He looked out over the moor and the clayworks, the trees of the grounds being sparse on this western side, their potency dissolving into the grimmer destructive mood beyond. The sky had a weird double tone — black rain-cloud overhead, the horizon pale as with a strange spreading corpse-light from the glare of the sun that was going down. The stacks and buildings of clayworks and the conical edges of the dunes were outlined against a bleared brightness, while the tops of trees near the manor were pushed upon the higher cloud-background. Beale brooded upon the chill scene, awaiting some movement that would check the sense of foreboding it inspired in him.

At length it came — the movement of two figures over a ridge of the downs, only a few hundred yards from the house, and approaching it. They walked some distance apart, but Beale soon recognized them, and a cruel smile broke softly, evilly upon his lips.

Timothy Cundy and Bert Truscott were hastening towards him, drawn by the lure of Florrie, the carnal heart of his power, now unclaimed and vulnerable.

Beale watched them hungrily; his hope rallied. As long as these men were loyal to him he could escape that final unveiling. The situation was not yet critical. A few weakly neurotic creatures might be sucked under the invading Shadow, but the intact virility of manhood was his.

Beale left the study and moved quickly along the

broad passage, that was dark. He heard Florrie opening the piano in the drawing-room, and reaching the door he knocked upon it and called:

'Your suitors have arrived!'

The door swung back and Florrie appeared, clad now in a blue evening gown, graceful and poisonous in the twilight.

'Both of them?' she asked with a swift flush of perverse sensuality.

'Yes. Almost at the door now. You'd better open it and welcome them yourself.'

Beale stood in the hall, very still and concentrated as he watched Florrie sway to the outer door. The clang of the manor gate reached him dully, then came the sound of rough male footsteps on the drive. They halted and the door-bell was rung.

Florrie opened the door quickly.

Timothy was there, a dark bulk of flesh towering up between the trees of the grounds and the ambiguous heaven. He wore his best suit, blue-grey tweed, and a black bowler. His purpose was obvious: he gazed at Florrie's rank female form with desire to possess and ravish it. He raised his hand to speak when Florrie interrupted him with a greeting.

'Well, Tim! This is no surprise. I know why you've come, both of you.'

As Beale stepped forward beside Florrie the second male figure appeared around a bend of the drive. Bert was dressed more roughly in grey flannel, a cap perched jauntily on his head, but his face bore the same aggressive stamp as Timothy's, even more lustful.

Timothy turned and shook his fist at Bert.

'No good coming here!' he shouted. 'I'm here first.'

'And you'll go first,' retorted Bert promptly. He

swaggered to the doorstep, his eyes challenging the young woman.

Florrie glanced about the grounds, fantastically dusked by the long sombre shadows of elms and beeches. The wind rasped and drained itself through the branches, flagging pettishly across to Florrie so that her frock whisked about her. She shrugged and laughed into Timothy's face.

'Let's all go in,' she said. 'We shall know then which of you has made a fool of himself.'

Beale led the way into the drawing-room. Timothy followed close at his heels, and after him, walking side by side, came Bert and Florrie.

As Florrie closed the door, Beale switched on the electric light and the fire, and at once a magical soft warmth and glow stole out, touching the cream walls, the furniture, and making even the two visitors seem less uncouth.

Removing their hats and holding them in their hands, Timothy and Bert seated themselves, at Florrie's request, on the divan, as far apart as possible, and eyed each other askance, warily. Beale and the girl took easy chairs that stood almost in the centre of the room. They turned their backs to the window, facing the visitors, and both smiled with veiled cruelty.

Timothy was the first to speak. He drew himself erect, folded his arms and fixed a piercing glance upon Florrie. He moistened his lips several times, jerking himself an inch backward with every appearance of his tongue.

'You know what's been developing,' began Timothy, 'and Ed have gone to clear the way for one or t'other of us. How've 'ee made up your mind? Which o' we two?'

He nodded at Bert to signify that the boxer was

108

present, though no attention should be paid to him. 'Which of us is the lucky man?'

Bert grinned broadly; his big, raw-boned face showed no concern. Although he could be sly on occasions his countenance was usually frank, boyish, and now its geniality contrasted sharply with the grim, dogged expression of Timothy's. He did not trouble to question the girl or comment on Timothy's remarks, but glanced at the tiger skin on the hearth, the piano standing across the opposite corner, his eyes darting presently back to Beale, at whom he winked with confident familiarity.

Florrie did not keep the three men long in suspense. She stretched a skinny arm towards Timothy, smiling with a cold, brittle enjoyment of her power to mortify him.

'I'm sorry, Timothy, but Bert's won the toss, I'm afraid. He had the first innings.'

Bert whistled, and rolling nearer to Timothy on the divan he prodded him in the ribs.

'There, old boy! Where's your brag now?'

Timothy rose and, with the aid of his hat, drew Florrie's attention more closely to his rival. He glared, the set of his face becoming for a moment formidable, and clenched his fists.

'What's Bert more than I, but a boozer?' he demanded wrathfully. 'Yes, and a man who never see a maid come evening time without taking her in claywork lane somewhere. If he don't burn down engine-houses 'tis only because he'll need 'em again for the next maid. A woman is blind what d'choose such trash when decent widowers is so plentiful in the room.'

Bert aimed a playful kick at the disgruntled Timothy, while the girl, with veiled wolfish malice, tried to soothe him.

'There's been a sort of agreement between me and

Bert for years,' she said, 'that if Ed did get fed up and desert me, Bert was to have what he wanted. Not a wife exactly: he isn't so innocent as you, Tim, to think it takes a wedding to fix things up. He'll be living here as my husband in everything but name. It'll suit us both: we aren't really the type for marriage.'

'But you led me to believe you was — damn 'ee!' shouted Timothy, walking round Florrie's chair to the piano and seating himself on the stool. ''Twas a decent wedded state we talked of a month ago. In this very house 'twas, when Beale was gone to a brewers' meeting. And you promised . . .'

Beale interrupted, quietly, leaning forward in his chair — he faced the fire and could with equal ease confront Bert or Timothy — and snapping his fingers.

'I think,' he said, 'there's something you both ought to know.'

Timothy scowled; he bit his tongue in perplexity, and before he could withdraw it Bert spoke.

'What's that?' enquired Bert.

Both men felt the presence of something ominous in Beale's remark. Even Bert looked troubled, guarded, his eyes half closed, as if he were in the ring awaiting his opponent's next move.

Beale glanced at Florrie, and as she nodded, evidently reading his desire and agreeing to it, he straightened and raised a hand, its rings glittering.

'Florrie,' declared Beale suavely, 'is not my daughter.'

There was a chilly silence while this news impressed itself upon the minds of Timothy and Bert, who now sat in opposite corners of the room. Both frowned, and Bert pushed a lock of hair impatiently from his eyes; he also wiped away sweat. Timothy again rose, and as Florrie's back was towards him he glowered at her head, swaying like a yellow flower on the long neck.

110

'Not your maid at all?' asked Timothy in bewilderment.

'Only by adoption. I was never married.' Beale's face twitched as he added grimly: 'Potter and I have been too busy fighting each other ever to think of marriage.'

'That don't tell much,' retorted Timothy, 'if we can believe all we heard o' Potter. When he ran the nunnery there by river bank there was plenty o' whispering about what happened to some o' they nuns.'

'Well, I'm not the daughter of a nun, either, I'm afraid,' laughed Florrie. She turned round in her seat, peering up at him over her shoulder. 'Mr Beale adopted me when I was a baby. But I'm no foreigner for all that. I was born not many miles from Carn Veor.'

'And whose brat was'ee?' demanded Timothy, on whom this news seemed to have had a more disconcerting effect than on Bert. 'Some come-be-chance, I s'pose — so low-born as your lout of a husband?'

Beale turned to Bert, who alone was now concerned in the issue.

'No,' said Beale with a strange sinister smile on his lips. 'Of all people in Carn Veor, Florrie is the one whose birth owes least to chance. Although I am not her father I am responsible for her existence.'

'How?' asked Bert in an awed tone.

Beale leaned towards him.

'You may remember hearing that some twenty-five years ago I was away from Carn Veor a considerable time?' he said.

'Yes — and better for us all if you'd never brought that back here,' cried Timothy, nodding at Florrie as at some alien, unclassified substance which he no longer recognized. 'Folks said you'd gone across river to carry on wi' some woman you'd got shut up there. Some said

111

'twas your true home where your wife was still living, and others said 'twas a bawdy-house you kept there.'

'Both of those ideas were wrong,' replied Beale cooly. 'I went back because it was necessary for me to supervise the enactment of a certain drama. Perhaps I should say "crime" — but that word is meaningless in Helburn pit . . . I cannot go into details, but there was something a little unnatural about the origin of Florrie. I knew that the production of a girl-child of a certain type would help me in my war against Potter. I selected her parents and assisted at every stage in the creation of the child.'

'Where was she born?' asked Timothy, subdued by the vague, unknown, ultimate powers loosed upon the room.

'On the bare sand of the clay-pit in which she was conceived — born of her mother as normally as your daughter Bronwen was born. There are no hospitals on my land across the river, and I took complete charge of the confinement. I will allow that the surroundings were very different from what is known here in the village. From neighbouring clay-pits there came sounds and smells that would have been terrifying to any villager. Occasionally explosions would rock the ground and waves of intense heat would sweep over us, setting up visual distortions so that hardly an object was recognizable and the woman lying on the clay-bed seemed no longer human. There would fall at intervals a scattering of black rain, hot as ashes from a volcano, and as it touched the woman she would scream out as though the pain of scorching was greater than the agony which the unborn child was causing her. The gangs of men and women who work for me in every one of those pits kept coming and going around us, but took no more notice of the naked, writhing woman than if she had been a dead rat. And in moments of silence as she laboured towards the birth and I knelt beside her, we could hear the wash of the river, the roar of the dark waters flowing between my secret pits and the open land on this side . . . But at last the child was born — a sickly girl; and the mother survived and suckled it as other infants are suckled, except that all happened within the walls of the clay-pit, amid the hot white slime that sometimes gushed from the rocks as if they too were turning to milk. When the child was weaned I took it and returned to Carn Veor, announcing her as my daughter and using her as I thought best to hasten Potter's defeat.'

'And Florrie ha'n't seen her mother since?' enquired Timothy, glowering in incredulous awe at Beale's strange story.

'No,' replied Beale. 'In that pit there are no human feelings: her mother has not missed her for a moment and would not know her if Florrie too crossed the dark river and rejoined the company among whom she was born.'

'Is her mother still alive?'

'Yes — as it happens, I've checked that point this afternoon. I phoned the asylum just now from Carn Veor office after my interview with the vicar. Florrie's mother is still an inmate, under constant guard for her own safety. She is a nymphomaniac, which may explain why Florrie should be — the Infernal Venus of the clay-lands, matching the Terrestrial Venus who lives somewhere nearer the church.'

'That's Rosa,' Florrie put in, searching Bert's face with jealous anxiety. 'Does this — make any difference?'

Her challenge renewed in Bert the sense of power and normality, though his gusto was a trifle strained.

'Not a bit,' he responded. 'You're the same maid you

113

always was — and there's few of us in Carn Veor who haven't had some daft ancestors!'

Florrie laughed as she rose and swayed across to the divan, seating herself beside Bert.

'Well, I'm glad this is settled,' observed Beale, lying back in his chair and adopting a more practical tone. 'I need a strong man from the clay-pits here to keep my Venus under control. If you decide to legalize the position later, I will see that Florrie gets her divorce.'

Timothy sat down upon the stool and scratched his head savagely. He was humiliated, reaching for some means of retaliation outside himself.

'Maybe 'tisn't settled,' remarked Timothy in his most mysterious tone. 'There's things happening what can upset plans a lot better laid than this one.'

Bert and Florrie were exchanging low pleasantries and paid no attention to him, but Beale's face showed an abrupt change, though he controlled himself and responded almost banteringly:

'You refer, I suppose, to the gossip of a certain Mrs Yelland?'

Timothy shouted his reply at the pair on the divan: 'Potter's Rock is something for 'ee to reckon with!'

Florrie's sickly face turned fully into the light: it had been screened by Bert's arm.

'That's nothing to us,' she said indifferently.

''Tis something to your father — stepfather or whatever he is. Isn't it Beale?'

Timothy wished at the next moment that he had been more discreet. Beale's countenance alarmed him; the ugliness of an inhuman tension darkened and distorted the squat simian features. Timothy drew back upon the stool, letting his hat fall to the floor.

While he was stooping for it Beale observed in a rapid undertone: 'If you have any advice to offer, either of you, I should be glad. I will admit to you that this matter is causing me some anxiety — far more than the loss of another engine-house. That can be remedied, but if the people of Carn Veor are drawn back to Potter's rule, if they succumb to the idiot propaganda of Mrs Yelland, then the loss to me is irreparable. I need all the help my friends can give me in stopping the rot. Something must be done before it spreads further.'

'You're taking it too serious — that's my advice,' said Bert with the spacious fluency of a man whose own worries have disappeared.

Timothy crossed a leg over his knee and shook his head. He addressed Beale gravely.

'Don't see you can do much, Beale. I thought Potter was on his last legs, but it seem they still got a kick in 'em. I hav'n't got no liking for the old blackguard meself — should be glad to see him finished — but if you'm to give him the knock-out you'll have to sharpen up your tools a bit.'

'Don't you listen to him, Mr Beale,' broke in Bert before Timothy had ceased speaking. 'He's got the blues through another sort o' knock-out — that's the point. There's nothing in this Rock business that need to frighten 'ee. What difference could it make to a fellow whose head was screwed on as 'a should be? I wouldn't mind going along just for fun to see what 'twas all about — and I'd be back to pub — or in a claywork lane as Tim says — same as ever the next evening.'

Beale turned to the boxer with a smile that showed the arousing of his malignant possessive instinct, recoiling and stiffening behind the urbane mask.

'You seriously think so, Mr Truscott?'

'Sure,' responded Bert, blinking up at the electric bulbs in the white panelled ceiling. 'All a man needs is guts — keeping his wits about'n and not getting

115

hysterics like a old woman. I'd expect a woman o' Mrs Yelland's age to be upset a bit by going in Potter's Lane. 'Tis a ghostly sort o' place, no doubt, wi' the few crooked trees you can see from the roadway and the waterlogged fields all around. I can fancy Mrs Yelland creeping through the lane, stopping dead every time she glimpsed they moonlight marshes. She'd think of all she heard about Potter being there hiding somewhere and how treacherous he was. She would feel like a body trapped and marooned in a strange land — nothing in sight to mind her of Carn Veor. By the time she got to the Rock she'd be in such a panic that she'd imagine things — start crying out to Potter maybe and making rash promises, as frightened women will. That's how it works — just the sense o' danger playing on the nerves. A few old noodles may be tricked by it, but they aren't much good to 'ee anyhow. The young ones'll never be drawed to Potter's Lane — and even if they went they'd only come back with a few more tricks to practise on your clayworks.' He turned to Timothy, the inquisitive gusto overriding the taunt in his voice.

'What about you, Tim? Would 'ee go along?'

Timothy rose and moved stiffly, sulkily towards the door.

'Don't say I would,' he muttered. 'Waste o' time — and maybe 'tisn't so safe either.'

'Not for you, p'raps. You've had your guts knocked out here tonight.'

'And soon it may be your turn. Now you got your young lady you may be too venturesome — if you aren't bluffing.'

'Oh, I aren't bluffing,' replied Bert. He pondered for a moment, his mind working quickly to decision. The three spectators watched him intently until he announced, straightening with an emphatic gesture:

'I'll prove to 'ee all that I'm as good as me word. *I'll go.*'

Beale gasped, and a shudder wrenched him. His flattened head jerked forward like a snake's, the blurred eyes strained defensively.

'In Potter's Lane? I wouldn't advise that, Mr Truscott. Cundy may be nearer the truth than you on some points.'

The boxer was undaunted, although he felt Florrie's arm quiver against his neck, the vibration of dread flowing in upon her from the deeps of Beale, the hidden potency that was threatened, almost maddened by Bert's resolve, yet remained unsuspected by the two men.

'I'll go along this very night,' Bert stated aggressively. 'Just for a joke — and to show Beale that they lighted matches in Rosa's trail is still the only thing he need worry about. I'll be back to Carn Veor pub tomorrow evening. Doings there then, isn't there?'

Florrie nodded: under cover of her hand she put her lips to Bert's, kissing him with that wolfish hunger which was now sharpened, panicky under vague menace.

'Sunday night special,' she murmured. 'You know what that means.'

'Sure. And this time 'twon't be just a tame little business o' skylarking wi' somebody. I'll give 'ee an account o' what I saw in Potter's Lane: we'll turn the meeting into a broadside against Mrs Yelland . . . You coming to listen, Tim?'

Timothy's reply was an angry word of farewell, and without glancing at Bert he left the room, slamming the outer door violently behind him.

It was now past six o'clock, almost dark. The moon would not rise yet for three hours, and the moor with its

117

bristling claywork angles was toned to a grim endurance of the interval of gloom as Timothy emerged from the grounds of Beale's home and fronted the open landscape. The wind howled dismally in the pits, blew in sharp nettling gusts about the stunted trees, and jabbed Timothy to a continuous strain of resistance. He pulled his hat low over his eyes, buttoned his coat and battled along the hedgeless road in lonely dignity.

His temper was ruffled, and he paid no attention to any detail of the twilit, gale-swept countryside. Except when the wind swirled full in his face, he kept his eyes fixed in a steady scowl on the cottages of Carn Veor, a shadowy outpost beside the white sprawling sand-dunes to the south. Even when passing the head of a lane that wound down to the gutted engine-house — a lane often used by lovers — he did not pause to ascertain whether any couples were now using it, drawn by the piquant sense that the ruins might serve them as the intact building had served Rosa and her partners.

A few hundred yards north of the Nances' home he was startled to observe a vague grey figure standing against a telegraph pole by the roadside. At first he thought it must be Rosa Nance waiting there for a lover, and his heart-beats quickened somewhat; he glanced furtively about. The humiliation he had suffered at Florrie's hands inclined him towards recklessness; he felt an urge for the dark potency that Rosa could restore to him. The challenge was almost on his lips when he perceived that the figure was not Rosa at all, but Maggie Gumma. Her hands were clasped tightly over her breasts, and below a green beret her face turned to him, white and flat like an elevated milestone.

Timothy glared at her, compelled to vent the coarse rage produced by these blunders.

'What the hell be sticked there for?' he demanded.

118

'You'll catch your death out in the freezing cold. Best go home and wait for doctor, you had.'

Maggie made no response; she remained stony, motionless, really unaware of him. Timothy swore at her and passed on.

There was no solace for him tonight, not even the practical sympathy of Bronwen. He arrived home to find the kitchen dark, the fire almost out and the lamp unlit. Bronwen was slumped at the table, huddled over it with her face smothered in her arms, crying bitterly.

Timothy was by this time in an exceedingly ill humour. He had stumbled over the carpet in the passage, and entered the room shaking his fist at the darkness. The discovery of Bronwen thus prostrated under her own troubles was a further jab that made this evening one which he long remembered for its plague of irritations.

Timothy had learnt from Joe in the afternoon — having met him while returning from the pump — that Joe's visit to Priory Bridge had been fruitless; and he had been unusually quiet at the tea table. He had watched his daughter critically almost the whole time — watched her staring with hard, smouldering rebellion out of the window. He had admired her grit, and was now vexed to find that her brave thrust of defiance had apparently lacked the stamina of fortitude.

''Nough o' your squalling — damn 'ee!' shouted Timothy, reaching her chair in one stride and roughly seizing her shoulders. 'You aren't the only one what've copped it tonight. Joe ha'n't got his work — no, nor he never will. You'll have to get 'ee out of your mind. And other things besides. All I've told 'ee about having to marry and clear out this summer. 'Tisn't true now. I've seen the bitch and she've changed her mind — throwed me over.'

119

Bronwen raised her eyes — weary, uncomprehending.

'You mean — Florrie Balker?'

'Who else?' he growled.

'Well, it don't matter now. Potter's as cruel as she is. 'Tis nothing but cruelty everywhere — Beale's side or Potter's, 'tis deception and cruelty the same. Better we was all dead!'

Chapter Eleven

WHEN Maggie Gumma left her home that evening the sun had set and the mood of night was encroaching — a cold, clammy, pagan night. Along the northern skyline the clay-dumps were no longer white or even grey cones, but mere flat shapes without feature. Those which still retained their pyramidal form were recognizable to the practised eye, but those that had swollen into irregular curves and angles were confused excrescences among low-lying black clouds. At first glance the clouds might have been mistaken for sand-dumps and the sand-dumps for clouds. Only by watching them for a few minutes until the clouds moved could even Maggie, in her present dulled state of mind, tell which was the natural and which the industrial blotch. And gradually the distinction vanished as a general wave of darkness welled up, spreading behind the clay-dumps, behind the clouds, so that all form and detail on or near the horizon became smudged, absorbed into the rising monotone of the background.

Instead of entering Carn Veor Maggie took a path through the down, west of the village, slanting towards the Nances' home. She slouched along mechanically, heavily, while her eyes groped and probed.

As she passed the vicarage the bedroom window opened and Mr Reed leaned out. He had come to his wife's room to switch on the light and draw the curtains, and wished to take a farewell view of the landscape before shutting himself in. He greeted Maggie pleasantly, but she stumbled on unheeding, without giving even a glance towards him. He watched her lurch to the roadway on the crest of the moor and saw her halt by the telegraph pole.

Maggie's thoughts as she leaned against the pole had a terrifying simplicity. They were one with the earth in their wretchedness, and wretched precisely because they were of the pagan earth that could breed without baptism and so made her burdened and vulnerable, dependent and slighted, a mere tool.

She remembered that she had once been a happy girl, scrambling about the sand-burrows in the winter twilight, the dusk that had then seemed crisp, unstained and friendly. She could not understand the process by which she had become her present self — this self that plumbed the menace of twilight, that projected a grey numbness upon the landscape so that she was confused, intermingled with it. The clay-dumps that had vanished from the sky-line seemed to be re-forming within herself. She felt the heaviness of clay, the gritty horror of refuse. It was as if she were a mere substance broken and spilled out over the flowers. But what had broken her, what was the rot from within that had made her brittle? George had coarsened, deadened her, but he too had once been intact, unflawed. There was a disintegration in them for which no external influence could account. They had not been warped by poverty or embittered by misfortune; they were not in essentials social products at all. Their own natures, in normal activity, had spun the web that was crushing them.

She might not have to bear its weight much longer. Only a few days — a week perhaps. Next Saturday there might be no such person as Maggie Gumma on earth. She accepted the possibility with stolid unconcern. Life and death were as blurred and intermingled as the dunes and clouds, both unreal now, something into which she had already dissolved.

Maggie had been standing nearly half-an-hour by the telegraph pole when Timothy passed. His appearance roused her somewhat, and after he had vanished behind the houses she moved stiffly into the road. No one else was visible; the village cowered, passive to the invasion of gloom — the harsh pagan gloom of the north. She stared at the church tower, which looked ineffectual; it was stiffened against the gloom but becoming as submerged by it as were the trees.

Maggie lurched towards the churchyard, where she would find shelter from the keen wind. Its wall was high, overleaned by a yew tree whose leaves rattled, though the sound was scarcely audible because of the distant dull clang of machinery in the clay-pits.

She had almost drawn level with the little iron gate when, glancing down the hill, she saw someone emerge from the Square and hurry towards her. The street was densely shadowed, and not until the figure was within a dozen yards of her did she recognize it was Rosa Nance.

A sharp gasp forced its way through Maggie's cold lips. She remembered, vaguely and painfully, the discussion in Mrs Budge's shop that afternoon, and found a momentary relief from her personal heaviness as she watched Rosa approach.

Rosa hurried forward, both arms outstretched, as if she were a child again, the child after baptism, grown beyond infancy to an awareness that was not yet a mature ebb and flow. She passed her home, came close up to Maggie and, laying a hand on her sleeve, greeted her with a warm smile, without speaking. Her eyes glowed, she looked upon the woman with a strange, piercing gaze.

Maggie drew back, sullen and a little fearful.

'What be staring at?' she mumbled. 'Be 'ee a witch now wi' your hair blowing so wild?'

123

Rosa shook her bare head.

'Not a witch, Maggie. I want to help you,' she replied.

A hard grunt escaped Maggie, her curiosity slowly arousing as she recalled the decision Rosa had announced a few hours before.

'Well — have 'ee been to Potter's Lane?'

'Yes, Maggie, I've been there.'

'And seen — same as Mrs Yelland — the Rock?'

Rosa looked fixedly up into the sky, her hands clasped.

'I've seen it,' she answered quietly; 'and my new life have begun as I hoped for.'

Maggie studied Rosa's face, studied it with something akin to awe. It was singularly beautiful, lifted in the half-darkness, the long golden hair tossing about it, flowing to the veiled breasts. The features had lost the coarse mould of habit; it seemed impossible that those parted lips could again be kissed lustfully.

'What be feeling like?' asked Maggie, fascinated.

Rosa made a gesture of passion.

'I couldn't put it into words: you wouldn't understand — or anybody. I can hardly get it clear myself yet. Only my bad life is gone — left down in the lane, buried under the Rock. Such thoughts have come, and I see why it is that we're all miserable.'

This was just what Maggie wished to hear, and clutching at Rosa's arm she drew her into the gateway.

'Tell me what you think,' she said.

Rosa glanced into the churchyard — indifferently, as if its pathetic peace no longer meant anything to her.

'When we aren't loving in Potter's way we're in Beale's shadow,' she replied, speaking slowly and deliberately. 'And here in the clay-lands Potter's way of love don't come natural to us. Our love is either downright wicked, like mine have been, or it's just pitiful, cheating us with false hopes, as Mrs Yelland said this afternoon. And so it grows as Beale would have it, whatever level we take it on.'

''Tisn't Beale who do harm us, 'tis the brutes we got to live with,' mumbled Maggie. 'Beale don't threaten me with 'is fist and order me outdoors like George did just now.'

Rosa searched the woman's puffy, sullen face, and saw her shiver as she gripped a spiked bar of the gate.

'You and George have had another quarrel?'

''Twas mother's fault again — 'tis always she who do aggravate George. When I got in from shop her corns was so bad she couldn't walk: nothing would content her but to bathe her feet. I told her to wait till after tea, but she's that pig-headed: nagging and nagging till I fetched the bath-pan and filled it with hot water. Her feet was still in the bath when George came home from work, and when he saw the table wasn't laid he went mad at us — pulled away the bath and threatened to tip the water over us if we didn't get his tea that minute. And so it went on — made me feel ill, and I was glad to be rid of 'em both.'

'I don't wonder, Maggie. But if you knew Potter's way of love — the secret of the Rock — the nightmare would break for you as it has for me and Mrs Yelland.'

Maggie blinked and scratched at her cheek; she was bewildered. It was hard to believe that this girl was the Rosa she had so often seen on the clayworks, moving towards some dump or building with a casual lover; the Rosa who normally treated her with gross familiarity. Mrs Yelland's report could not be fanciful: Rosa had gone to Potter's Lane in a mood of passion, not of sober curiosity, yet a similar mysterious change had come upon her through the spell of the Rock. Perhaps they had both reached a point where suffering had bared them to Potter's will; and Maggie too was near such a crisis. Through the sluggishness of the breeding body she was aware of stirrings within and beyond the clay barrier.

Maggie looked stonily for a few minutes past the pump, down the slope to her home, where lamplight flowed steadily through the window. She glanced then across the moor at the clay-tanks, drying-sheds and stacks pouring smoke and soot over the white, smouldering heaps of soil. She gave suddenly a little whimper of pain, pressed a fist on her belly and turned her face to the wall shadowed by the yew tree.

'I dunno what to do,' she moaned. 'I can't have love, no odds where I go to. George won't be kind to me nor kiss me any more; 'tis his fist I'll be tasting if I aren't careful. Now I'm heavy wi' me baby he could kill me at a blow, but he don't think — he wouldn't think in time when he was in a temper. I'd be on the floor dying in a miscarriage before he knew what he'd done.'

'Maggie, I do feel for you — I do. It's worse when you wake up to the cruel truth *after* you're married: you feel you can't escape by finding some different sort o' man. But you can get rid of all these fears, even as you are — and maybe draw George along with you.'

Maggie peered at Rosa and enquired in a dull tone: 'What sort of rock is it, this strange one o' Potter's?'

Rosa stepped into the road, a sharp gust of wind stinging her face with gravel licked up from the gutter, so that she raised a hand to shield herself and half turned.

'It's white — clay rock, like you see blasted in the pits,' she said as the wind lulled. 'But the *feel* of it . . . I can't tell you how different 'tis. You feel as if it's *alive* — as if Potter's love is pouring into it, and as you stand and let its shadow cover you — the power sinks in and — and you feel ashamed.'

'Ashamed, Rosa? Why should 'ee be ashamed because Potter chooses to bring a old rock across the river and dump it down in his lane?'

'You know it doesn't belong over here,' replied Rosa quietly, 'with the smoke from Beale's stacks blowing down towards it and the thorns scraping at it all the time. Potter treasures it above everything — you *feel* he does — yet he put it there to help us, showing that his way of love is strange and different from ours.'

''Tis only to get his own back on Beale,' said Maggie scornfully.

Rosa turned towards her home, opposite the church-yard, wishing to hide her face from Maggie as a quick revulsion of feeling flooded her. She had felt the presence of Beale in the lane, terribly threatening, and only after a long struggle of her will had she gone forward, beyond the point where Beale had seduced her until she saw the Rock. She stretched her arms now towards the clayworks; and as if in malicious response there came a sudden blinding glare of light, a score of white jets spurting at scattered points as the electric current was switched on — some on the clay-tips far up against the sky, some lower down on the tank walls, others at ground level beside the micas, and many in the pits, so that the light itself was invisible here, only the diffused reflection staining the skyline as a phosphor-escent background for the upper lights. Rosa made a gesture as though to push them aside, to thrust them back, with the tormenting reminders they brought to her. That had been her world until tonight: those lights had been her signal, they had winked blearedly over the shadowy, obscene figures of the men tumbling to her through the mud. The lights had mingled with her

127

carnal flame, discovered her. They pulled now, they seemed to strike at her, as if they were emanations of Beale, and somehow famished. She closed her eyes, finding release in the mental image, the last bend of the lane, the Rock in the field. Presently she turned back to Maggie.

'Beale's the enemy of us all,' she said, her voice strained and defensive, 'and every time Potter scores over him we're safer. There's no hope for us till Beale's shadow is driven from our lives. And only the Rock can take it away, for Beale lives close to us and is mixed up with everything.'

Maggie was about to reply when a dark figure loomed across the road, someone whom they had not heard approaching. It was a woman, tall but drooping, with the angularities of a sapless middle age in her grey-clad contours. She had emerged from a side street near the village square.

Rosa impulsively stepped towards her.

'Oh — Miss Pascoe!' she exclaimed. 'I'm glad to see you as well. It's true, isn't it, that you went after Mrs Yelland last Sunday — down to Potter's Lane? I've just been . . .'

Miss Pascoe quickened her pace, almost running towards the gateway of her home on the lower side of the pump. Rosa and Maggie watched her in perplexity as, without speaking, she entered the house, slamming the door behind her.

'That's queer!' commented Rosa.

Maggie shook herself and moved heavily into the road. A strong eddy of wind struck her and she stumbled against Rosa, staring at the girl, her mind confused, slipping back into its main bewilderment about Rosa herself.

'You'm the last person I should have thought to hear

speak a good word for Potter,' she mumbled. 'I've always heard he's terrible hard on a maid when she've gone wrong and done what she oughtn't with her body.'

Rosa smiled, taking Maggie's arm in a firm grasp.

'That's a lie like the rest,' she said. 'All that's reported o' Potter in Carn Veor is lies — Beale's lies.'

'P'raps 'tis,' remarked Maggie. 'But that don't make things easier for me.'

Rosa tugged persuasively at Maggie's sleeve.

'You know I said I wanted to help you. Why not go along like I have? 'Twould put new life into you, I'm sure 'twould. Just come along with me tonight: you can walk that far I expect, if we go slow.'

Maggie blinked up at the sky and the church tower. She saw George's face frowning at her in the clouds, the human menace projected, Nature unified against her. She bit her lip.

'I'd like just to have a look at'n,' she said huskily. 'Must be something good I should think, to make 'ee so glad. But I dunno if Potter would like me to come as I be now. 'Twould tell too much. If he should be there looking . . .'

'He will be,' admitted Rosa. 'I knew he was there all the time I was in the lane; only he don't show himself.'

'I don't want Potter to see me in this state,' Maggie objected, hesitant and fretful as the old instinctive dread returned upon her.

'It wouldn't make any difference — even if you wasn't married. It isn't *that* you'll be ashamed of down there. And it shows how much you need love, and the more you need it the gladder Potter'll be when you come to see the Rock . . . Do come, Maggie! 'Tis your only chance.'

Her eyes besought Maggie, who pondered for several minutes, her hands clenched above her unborn child.

129

Darkness had settled now on the village, though the claywork lights were becoming more distinct and potent beyond it. The wind had lulled, but the sense of calm was uneasy, ominous. A yellow flare from an oil lamp kindled in Miss Pascoe's window. Maggie glimpsed it and an agony of desire burned within her — as compelling as that which Rosa had felt, but different in kind, for it was an experience entirely new to her, an abrupt invasion, not the tormenting climax of a conflict that had burdened and pulled upon her from childhood. But it soon mastered the scruples of her instinct and reason; her hand groped timidly to Rosa's.

'I'll go with 'ee,' she said.

Chapter Twelve

MR REED awoke the next morning in a mood of vague fragile hope. He had slept well, relaxed and fulfilled within himself. His wife had shown him a little kindness after he watched Maggie's approach to the church-yard. For the first time since settling at the vicarage he had not been obliged to sleep in a separate room, but shared the front room bed lawfully with Mrs Reed. Such an experience had been so rare during the closing months of his ministry in Essex that he regarded it as a favourable omen. If his wife thus solaced him and Beale helped him openly, some good work might be done here. It really depended on Beale. He felt that even this sudden itch of desire in his wife was in part an outcome of his meeting with Beale. The spirit of Beale had marked him deeply, burnt into him with the overtones of drama and excitement in the blazing engine-house. Mrs Reed had scented the fresh tang, the subtle change in his personality: she had been curious and greedy about it, and the vicar had been surprised and troubled by her sudden warmth. He had felt that she was not acting on a healthy natural impulse but under strong hypnotic influence, a dark psychic control exerted by Beale.

Mrs Reed was still asleep, her face looking strangely flushed and gross under the sweaty grey hair. Her hus-band watched her furtively and rather uneasily as he dressed, and then crossed to the window, seeking from the wider field of Nature a refreshment for the tasks of the coming day — the first Sunday of his ministry in the village. The dawn was slowly pressing up from the east, a brilliant spring dawn, and it fascinated him because of the awareness Beale had brought him, the complex spiritual intimations. He could not view it in the simple, naturalistic manner in which he had viewed so many dawns in Essex. It was not just a fine morning of an early English spring, but, like the landscape it transfigured, a thing of apocalypse and symbolism.

The dawn revealed paganism in a new mood, no longer cold and sullen, but riotous, vivid with fecundity, a massive foaming up of rebellion in colour and warm kindling light. There was a deliberation and eagerness in the first running waves of sunshine; they did not grope or flounder through cloud, or steal gently along the fields, but struck with sudden blinding darts the peaks of the sand-dumps, setting the electric wires gleaming like spiders' webs against the pale blue sky and enveloping the tip-beams in a fervid radiance so that iron fastenings breaking their dull grained surface were plainly visible from below. The ardent unresisted wave peeled off the shadows from the cones before it touched the natural landscape; its first communion was with the clay, and the flowers had to wait in frosty twilight while the refuse-heaps, scarred and drained beyond fertility, shared in the splendour of the pagan challenge, as if aware of themselves as offspring of the will of Beale.

As Mr Reed looked upon this tide of sunlight heaving forward to Beale's home, it seemed to him that he was watching something obscene. The manor was in grey shade as yet, very remote in the smoky northern dusk, but its trees were stiff and full of a strange potency that awaited the touch of the advancing dawn. The power of the manor seemed to be pulling the light wave towards itself; that dark spot on the distant moor was as a womb upon which the life of the dawn was focussed. When the sunbeams spilled among its trees, flowed against its windows and eddied into the rooms where Beale breathed and planned, there would be a fecundity in the mingling, a fusion of the light of Nature and the darkness of Beale. And in that union he, the vicar, had a part now; he must turn to it for strength and support. In himself he was completely drained of vitality; the alien, oppressive land, the sullen brutality of the people, bewildered and exhausted him. He groped blindly and instinctively towards the beauty of the spring dawn, the rich poetry of the earth, thrilling as it raced over the convulsions and scars of the material world to quicken the spirit at its heart. For Beale was the spiritual heart; the manor was the generating house that fed the schools and churches of the clay-lands and gave life to all movements of human religion outside Potter's Lane.

Mr Reed recalled his talk with Beale in the claywork office. He felt a slight inflow of assurance, though the scene was fantastic in his memory; the lurid background of the fire down by the clay-pit at which Beale had looked with inhuman indifference as he spoke of his real warfare, his inscrutable adversary. The situation still troubled the vicar's mind, so utterly foreign was it to the peaceful routine of a country parish in which he had expected to be immersed. If he could tap the depth of Beale's power, it would probably yield him enough energy for his immediate purpose, but his fate was now linked with Beale's, and only in Beale's final triumph could he find security. And was the power of the manor sufficient for that task, even when impregnated by Nature? Carn Veor might be freed from superstition by the broad, healthy tides of progressive thought, but when they flowed on and encountered the barrier beyond the barrier of clay, the thorn trees of Potter's Lane — what then? Beale himself seemed to fear that

133

they would always be turned back at that point. The manor was not the only source of power in the district. There was Potter's Lane — and there were other places even more mysteriously shrouded . . .

Mr Reed glanced at a newspaper lying on the dressing table, and at once frowned, reminded of an item that had disturbed him when he first read it last evening. It was a poem describing the strange happenings at a place called Pentroth Pit. Wherever this might be, the lines suggested that a sinister confederacy was ranged against the forces of enlightenment in this primitive heart of Cornwall:

> 'For Potter still may pace the peak
>   Where tip-beams like huge crosses break
> The Cornish landscape into dim
>   Avowals that we martyred him . . .'

The odd thing was that, read here inside the clay country, the poem did not seem unreal or fantastic. He felt that Potter and his unknown agents might very well be plotting dark things amid the refuse of some hidden pit, even now while the spring dawn was cleansing the earth, pulsing and flooding among the white pyramids, the stacks and faint tufts of smoke, ever nearer to Beale's home. Potter may have suffered a spiritual martyrdom, but he was still alive, wily and unscrupulous. The vicar yearned for Beale's protection, feeling the unseen terror that was abroad, the alien, transmuting power which threatened to bring a flagging to the heart of every sunbeam as it moved out, unguarded and vulnerable, towards the manor.

Mr Reed opened the high, narrow window and leaned over the sill. The window faced north-east and the shadow of the house stretched coldly across the lawns almost to the road. There was a slight tang of frost, a keen rasp in the wind that flicked at the curtain. Rooks were cawing among the elms of the drive, and occasionally one flapped over the vicarage roof. Sparrows also darted and twittered, bringing material to their nests in the eaves. But there was a stain upon the melody of the dawn as upon its visible wave. The pure chorus of skylarks was blunted by the raucous crowing of cocks in George Gumma's fowl-house. And though the clay-works were not fully active the familiar grating and chugging noises broke squalidly from various quarters of the moor.

The vicar looked wistfully towards the church, where he would soon be taking the first morning service. It reminded him of the human element, the material which he must actually grapple with and seek to mould. He watched the strip of open road beyond the last block of houses, and presently observed signs that the village was awakening, the people astir against the surging tensions of the background.

He was surprised, first of all, to see Joe Gool emerge on the hilltop, trundling a wheelbarrow in which a shovel had been placed. Joe turned the corner by the office and then branched off from the lane, pushing the barrow across the field towards the low refuse-dumps above the gutted engine-house. He moved wearily, his shoulders drooping, and the vicar felt almost a twinge of pity as he compared this abject mood with the jocular, assured manner Joe had shown yesterday when chatting with him on the sandbanks. He had learned last evening of Joe's failure at Priory Bridge, and the news fitted in with the view he had already formed of Potter's character. He saw the young man now distortedly as a creature jerking back into crude neutrality after his brief, abortive grapple with the unseen. The stumbling figure clutching at the barrow, pressing its iron wheel over the

135

daisies of the field, was a symbol of mere human brutality, cast out from Potter's world but untouched by the spirit of worship that remained in Nature.

When Joe had disappeared the vicar's attention was caught by a further disturbing movement. The burly, gleaming form of PC Rodda arose from the shadow of the Nances' garden, vaulted over the low wall and entered the road. He stepped past the church, and looked at it furtively and resentfully. Mr Reed had heard enough about the constable to guess the meaning of this behaviour. He knew that Rodda was not awaiting the emergence of some village lecher so that he could charge the Nances with keeping a disorderly house. He had wished to be admitted himself, to celebrate the pagan dawn with the harlot.

Mr Reed sighed as he watched the black uniformed figure, so obscene in its bafflement. It was just another proof of the moral corruption which pressed down upon him on every hand. What could his puny efforts avail in a village where even the officer of the law was a flagrant offender against the most elementary decencies of society? And what support could be received from Beale, who knew of this corruption, yet made no protest? Beale was the enigma at the *heart* of this incredible situation.

The vicar fidgeted nervously with his clerical collar. He drew back from the window, peering westward at the Gummas' home. It stood full in the wash of sunrise, a sort of oasis of nostalgic release for Mr Reed. The dumpy, cosy little place brought him a moment's vision of the normal, simple life of the land, the farmlands and orchards beyond Langley, looking north to the borders of Hertfordshire. His face relaxed dreamily as he fused the past scenes of rural peace with the deep inner sense of fulfilment which his wife had given him here last night. But as the fusion became conscious it repelled him, for the erotic element was the stronger, and it gripped him to the clayworks, to the flame of the engine-house, and to Beale. And before he could dissolve the fusion the dark colouring of Beale had spread over the old pastoral innocence. It was as if he had always vaguely known Beale, even while living in Essex; as if for ten years he had been watching for Beale's movements in the fields around Saffron Walden, listening for Beale's footsteps on the village roads . . .

The nightmare fell from him, broken by the sound of other footsteps — clear, brisk footsteps approaching from without, from beyond the Gummas' cottage. Along the road from the west a man was drawing near, utterly removed in tone and significance from the two he had just seen on the hilltop. The man was as burly as the constable and as careless about appearances as Joe, but there was nothing of stealth or tiredness in his firm, swinging stride. He whistled as he walked, glancing about with a vivid gusto of enjoyment and taking the sunlight full on his big, uplifted face. Mr Reed soon recognized him as Bert Truscott.

When he was abreast of the vicarage Bert sighted the vicar inside the bedroom window, and raised his cap respectfully.

''Morning, sir!'

The vicar nodded stiffly.

'Good morning!' he said shrinking from the warmth of Bert's manner, and misreading it. General gossip had left him in no doubt that Bert was an even greater menace than Rodda to the moral stability of the village.

Bert seemed to hestitate for a few seconds, moistening his lips, then remarked tentatively:

'Starting your work here today, I believe?'

'I am,' replied the vicar.

'Well, you'll have a easier job than you bargained for, by the look of it.'

'I beg your pardon?'

'You'd have found the young folks a tight handful, I'm afraid, if my influence was still pulling Beale's way,' said Bert with a chuckle. 'But me and you together, sir, wi' Potter behind us . . .'

Mr Reed slammed the window, and Bert looked nonplussed for a minute, staring at the closed panes in surprise, then strolled on towards the village in a slightly more subdued mood.

The banging of the window had awakened Mrs Reed; a sound from the bed distracted the vicar from the mysterious implication of Bert's remarks. He looked around at his wife guardedly, adjusting himself, intimately aware of her.

But there was no contact; the spell was gone. The wrenched face was hostile and distant, reared snake-like on the pillow as he had seen it so often before he encountered Beale. He smiled and approached her, but she made a gesture of repugnance. Her voice came shrilly conveying the old neurosis, the sense of outrage.

'Felix! What are you doing in my room?'

His hand fumbled to the bed-rail.

'Why — my dear — surely you remember . . . ?'

'I remember nothing,' she said coldly. 'Will you leave the room and allow me to dress?'

He blinked at her through his spectacles for a few moments, then went out with his head bent, mortified. He understood. He had not yet received enough of the spirit of Beale, the inhuman fascination, to hold her for long.

Chapter Thirteen

BERT TRUSCOTT had risen early that morning and left home while his parents were still asleep. Before the cold twilight began to dissolve he had hurried across the moor to the western end of Potter's Lane. He had touched the stones at the mouth of the lane, standing with bowed head as daylight flooded in, bringing the assurance that his experience here last night was real and not a dream. He had felt the power of the lane sweep up against the pagan power of the dawn and hold it steadily, draining it of pride. The little dawn, cramped and captive within the spiritual daybreak, was subdued for Bert; it was forced to minister to the new life within him, though in its own nature it was hostile. All that the vicar had sensed and recoiled from, Bert welcomed as proof of the supremacy of the Power to which he had yielded.

Bert respected force; it was almost the only thing he did respect, in himself or in others. He was proud that his hands, when they formed fists inside padded gloves, could knock down the biggest and toughest men in the clay district, and that the same hands, when bare, could bring a girl to the point of carnal surrender. His life passed in a rhythm of mastery — mastery over men in fights — mastery over girls in embraces. It was the only nerve in him that was sensitive, the only idiom he understood. The world of subtlety and intelligence had never touched him; he had been contemptuous of spiritual values and religious ideas because he had believed that they belonged to this elegant world and were not crude forces that he could respect. If ever the spiritual side of life aroused his interest it would have to use a very different, a barbaric and inhuman language: he would recognize it only if he were hit by it.

He had known as he left Beale's manor last night that an encounter of this sort was imminent. He had gone to Potter's Lane expecting a minor battle of nerves — a battle which he could win as easily as he might win a physical combat with a light-weight opponent. But the unseen adversary had taken his measure; the adversary was a colossus. Bert had been trapped and out-manoeuvred, and had at length staggered from the lane more thoroughly shaken and routed than he had ever been when leaving a boxing ring and yet filled with a glow of liberation and wellbeing greater than anything he had felt after ravishing a girl. He understood, dimly and wonderingly, that he had not gone to the lane on a mere whimsical impulse of his own. The will of Potter had invaded Beale's home last evening, invaded the room where Beale sat with him, and marked him as the next captive who must be freed.

Bert's was not a nature that could keep a good thing to itself. He could not repress his joy and amazement; they bubbled up to his lips and set him whistling and humming as he strode buoyantly back to Carn Veor. He wished to share his exuberant zest with others.

On sighting Mr Reed at his window Bert had felt that it was fitting that the vicar should be the first to hear of his experience. In his simplicity Bert thought the clergy-man would be glad to learn of the spiritual change that had come to him in Potter's Lane, and would give him some wise counsel regarding the nurture of this new life. But he had been disappointed. Mr Reed was obviously in no mood to listen to his tale, and it seemed probable that he never was in such a mood. Bert was a little perplexed and sorry for the vicar, but not

troubled on his own account. If Mr Reed did not
respect force there were plenty of people in Carn Veor
who did.

When he entered the Square, however, he found it
deserted except for a black cat sitting on the memorial
steps and a terrier that was scratching itself outside
the Cundy's gateway. The church clock had only just
struck seven, and the usual Sunday morning drowsi-
ness of the village was not yet disturbed. Curtains were
still drawn over many bedroom windows, most doors
were closed and locked, and the sky above the house
roofs was unstained by smoke. A smell of frying bacon
permeated the corner by the outer street, issuing
through the Yelland's open door-way; and being thus
reminded of Mrs Yelland Bert paused, uncertain
whether he should call on her before making any
general confession.

While he debated the point, Yelland himself came
lumbering around the corner into the Square. He
moved slowly, a grey bulk in the cool shadow, puffing
his pipe. Bert peered at him in surprise, feeling the
strangeness, as if the new day were being patterned and
all movements about him were controlled and signifi-
cant.

'Good morning, Bert!' Yelland greeted. 'You're out
early.'

'I've been out nearly all night,' replied Bert.

'I can guess where, I believe.'

'Maybe you're wrong. I didn't go to bed till three
o'clock and now daylight's come — well, I feel I must be
seeing Carn Veor as 'twas before Beale came here. Like
a new world, all this mucky little place.'

'That'll wear off when you get sober, Bert?'

'I'm soberest body in Carn Veor this morning —
except your missus and Ellen Pascoe perhaps.'

Yelland stared, faintly grasping the hint, but incredulous.

'Eh? Where've you been? We thought you was out seeing Florrie last night.'

'So I was, but it didn' end there. I got a tale to tell what'll give folks here a bigger kick than they've had for years.'

PC Rodda had been lingering in the road that led past the church since Mr Reed saw him leave Rosa's home. Hearing Bert's voice — a loud one normally, and now he was shouting — Rodda came bristly downhill into the Square. He still looked sulky and betrayed annoyance as he enquired:

'What's on, Truscott?'

Bert turned, lifting his hand respectfully.

'No law agin talking, is there?' he said.

The constable's eyes narrowed suspiciously.

'Oh, I aren't drunk,' Bert assured him. He swung up on to a step of the monument, causing the cat to retreat stiffly to the opposite ditch.

Rodda crossed to the gateway of his home, not far from the Cundys', and adjusting his helmet he awaited developments with a morose curiosity.

Yelland approached the memorial.

'Let's hear your news, Bert,' he said after some hesitation.

'Can't 'ee guess what 'tis?'

'If you'd seen my woman and been dinned in the ears all the week like I have, I could guess right enough,' Yelland replied. 'But they two at the manor wouldn't give 'ee a send-off in that direction.'

'You don't need send-offs when your time comes,' said Bert. 'Anyhow, I've took the same step as your missus, and want to tell 'ee how it've worked in my case.'

142

At this announcement, given with challenging gusto, the Cundy's door opened and Timothy appeared. Bronwen was still asleep, and while lighting the kitchen fire — which had been obstinate, compelling him to waste nearly half a pint of paraffin — Timothy had noted Bert's arrival with dark feelings of enmity. He now spoke in a jeering tone:

'So you did go along, Bert? Seen the old Rock?'

'Sure.'

'And how've it turned out?'

'Just like you said 'twould. You'm a true prophet, Tim — but I only regret you wasn't there with me.'

Timothy leaned against the door-post and folded his arms; his face, however, showed that deep personal excitement had begun to well in him. He looked expectant, vaguely hopeful, though still contemptuous in his steady glare at Bert.

Sounds of activity within doors — the click of locks and rattle of window sashes — encouraged Bert to proceed with his recital.

'Ed Balker's behind this, as he's behind that claywork blaze yesterday,' Bert explained to his unseen audience. 'I had to nip in quick after Ed was gone. But things went too smooth and put me in a mood to dare anything and show off: I felt I could take on all comers, and told Beale and Florrie — and Tim Cundy was there listening too — that I'd go along to Potter's Lane just for a joke. But I know now 'twas Potter drawing me. I got to take back all me boasting. 'Twasn't no old woman's nerves that made Mrs Yelland give in. I've had the biggest battle o' me life tonight: I've been hit below the belt and between the eyes — I've been down for the count — down on my knees; yet somehow I know I've *won* the battle. That's the point.'

While Yelland gaped at Bert with stolid fascination

Timothy weighed Bert's words; he let their implication feed his excitement, which soon reached a pressure that forced from him a decisive question.

'Who's goin' to have Florrie?' he demanded, stepping down to the gate in a tense, suppressed attitude. His short ginger hair was uncombed, and stuck up aggressively on his large bony head.

'Not me,' replied Bert in a more subdued tone. 'Best keep your mouth shut, Tim, about what you heard at the manor last evening.'

Timothy spat derisively, but a grim satisfaction was settling upon him; his thoughts were burrowing back towards the point from which they had recently been dislodged.

'So the meeting at the pub tonight'll be tame after all,' he taunted. 'No broadside agin Mrs Yelland like you promised us.'

'No; me broadside's going to be fired off here,' said Bert, 'straight agin Beale hisself.'

Bert's visible audience was increasing rapidly. Almost every house in the Square showed someone on a doorstep or leaning out of a bedroom window. Those standing in doorways on the western side of the street craned their necks to see around the body of the monument. All recognized the speaker; all knew that something extraordinary had occurred; all listened.

'Beale didn't want me to go along,' Bert continued, watching Timothy, who was now leaning over the gate and looking dubiously at Rodda. 'I knew he was scared stiff, though he tried not to show it. And he got good cause to be scared now there's Potter's Rock to be reckoned with.'

Mrs Rickard, the Cundys' next-door neighbour — an amazingly fat lady with bobbed grey hair and a nose that bulged like a little crimson balloon — now ap-

peared at her bedroom window. She addressed Mrs
Tabb, a middle-aged consumptive who occupied the
next window on the left.

''Tis a queer week-end, Mrs Tabb: first our engine-
house going up in flames, and now Bert adding fuel to
Mrs Yelland.'

'Aye,' retorted Bert genially, a broad grin spreading
across his face. 'We'll burn up everything that belongs
to Beale before we've finished. That's Potter's aim all
right. All the bad doings that make our village a byword
have got to be scorched up by the fire from Potter's
Lane.'

A dowdily-dressed woman bawled from behind him:

'Carn Veor's no worse than other places, Bert: you
needn't go fouling your own nest.'

Bert turned to glance at the woman, but ignored her
interruption.

'All the place here is gone soft,' he resumed earnestly.
'We think we're a tough-living lot with our grabbing
and squabbling and carrying on here and there. But 'tis
soft, flabby living that's dried away to nothing the
moment you feel the life o' the Rock.'

Bert paused, then as no-one offered any comment he
moved sideways to the edge of the step and swept his
arm in a passionate gesture.

'How long shall us wait for Potter's rule to come and
harden us up out of our slushy ways?' he demanded.
'There's only one way to bring it — to fetch it up from
Potter's Lane in our hearts like me and Mrs Yelland
have done. We can't work it up inside Beale's boun-
daries. It's a fool's game to sow your wild oats instead o'
going to Potter's Lane, but it's just as big a folly to try
and mend your ways here instead o' going to Potter's
Lane. When he says "Go there", whatever you do
instead o' that is a twist and a wash-out.'

145

'Parson Bully didn't think so,' cried Mrs Tabb.

'I know he didn't,' agreed Bert, cocking his eye with a twinkle of reminiscence towards her window; 'and I know he was a fool. Bully must take his share o' the blame for the mess we're in. We've lost touch wi' Potter ever since that fellow came here and spied on the Rock. He said 'twas only a bit o' blasted stone that Potter had stole from some quarry and palmed off as a old Stone o' Sacrifice wi' magic in it. But Bully was wrong. The power we need is down there in the valley and nowhere else. Our only hope is in doing the one simple thing that Potter demands. Go down to that lane. Feel the stab o' they thorn trees. Fight through to the Rock. That's where Potter's grip begins — and it's reaching Carn Veor again. The battle is on and we've all got to take what's coming to us.'

Chapter Fourteen

BERT ended on a subdued note, though he had bawled some of the earlier sentences. It was as if he were tensing himself, aware of an approaching menace. The hostile element among the crowd was strong; the spirit of Beale was moving, stiffening the figures, hardening the faces against him. He had expected this and was not troubled by it. But in the silence that now fell upon the Square there was something else, a tenseness sharp and nerve-racking — the sense of the near presence of the living heart of Beale, the massive swooping of the dark heart against the boxer's defiance.

Bert felt the chill, inhuman invasion, but he did not flinch, even when he heard the footsteps, the low excited cries from the upper end of the Square, and then saw her appear — the lean, white-garbed figure of Florrie, moving towards him.

She entered the Square deliberately, her eyes darting at once to the man on the step of the monument, seizing upon him with a cold, deadly challenge. She was heedless of the fixed attention of the crowd, passing the groups unseeingly, even when they broke up to make a path for her. She did not observe Rodda edging stiffly out from his gateway with a look of baffled concern on his face, and she would not have been deflected from her purpose had she seen him. She knew he would not dare to interfere in such a matter as this. He took his orders from Beale, he acted in affairs that concerned the outside everyday world. But this was different. She and Bert were isolated, enclosed in a private battle area of the flesh and spirit.

Bert had shifted, turned a little to meet her, his arms hanging loosely, his face pale, grim. His look was that of one who accepted the situation as inevitable, something he had brought upon himself and must surmount. He closed his eyes for a moment, as if in prayer.

Florrie reached the base of the steps and halted. She looked more wolfish than ever, her out-thrusting teeth bared in a snarl, her green eyes narrowed to flashing fiery slits that bored cruelly into his.

For a few minutes there was an awesome hush, while the sunlight, flooding above the house roofs, sent its first eddies into the Square, kindling the grey stone head of the cross to a ruddy and sinister sharpness of detail, slipping in broad prongs to the tensed figures below: Bert's dark, warm, burly, the woman's white and cold and emaciated. The striking of these sunbeams was like the sudden glare of a spotlight on an arena; and the pitiless conflict opened immediately. Florrie went straight to its heart without preliminaries.

'You bastard!' she cried, her voice coming at him with a low hiss of hatred. 'Didn't I warn you what would happen if you went there?'

Bert steadied himself against the cross, nodding slowly.

'I know,' he replied, his tone fumbling up through the shame of memory to a quiet firmness of triumph. 'I was a fool to believe you and Beale could protect me when Potter's hour struck. But the nightmare's broke now.'

'Your love for me — a nightmare?'

'What else could it be when Beale sheltered it?'

She probed his features, seeking the clue to the change in him, but completely baffled. The features were subtly different, expressing a new spirit, but they were as strong and rugged as ever. The virility re-

148

mained, but its essence had become alien, beyond her.

'What the hell *is* it that happens in that lane?' she demanded. 'What *are* you? Aren't you a man any more?'

'I aren't Bert Truscott — not the bloke you clung to last night after Tim left the manor,' responded Bert, recoiling from the maddened, snout-like face that was trying to break into him and feed on him. 'Don't ask me to explain. Your — dad or whatever he is — knows more about it than I do.'

'We knew you were like a blind man walking over a cliff. We knew you'd come back — burnt out as you are, and no good to me. But what's left to you now?'

'Something better than I've ever had from you.'

'Don't you see how you've been tricked?'

'No, it isn't any trick,' said Bert.

She leaned forward, her hollow flanks gripped with the primitive antagonism.

'You've thrown me over — I knew you would,' she continued hoarsely. 'But for what? For a cold Rock in a field?'

'That's the beginning all right,' admitted Bert, glancing aside at the still, fascinated groups to ease the pressure of the duel. 'I can't tell yet what it may lead to: I shall read Potter's book and find out. But I do know it leads away from you — away from Beale and everything he's left his mark upon.'

Florrie stepped back, releasing her whole personality to weaken him, to rouse the old, brutal manhood in him for a death-grapple.

'But you can't just drift off on your own. You can't be neutral. You know what it means. You're fighting us now.'

Bert held off the pressure, but was strained by it. His hands trembled slightly, and he moistened his lips.

149

'I'm waiting Potter's orders about my next move,' he said, almost muttering the words. 'But I daresay you're right. I aren't being neutral in standing here.'

'You're defying us?'

'I'm as bad as Mrs Yelland, I daresay.'

'You're defying us?'

'It looks like it.'

'Well, I don't know what dad may do. He doesn't feel the *woman's* side of this struggle. To have left me for another girl would have been bad enough, but — for that lane — for *him* . . .'

Bert shuffled his feet, but his answer came without hesitation or apology.

'I admit I've gone back on my word, but I only gave it because I was Beale's, body and soul — yours because his. And now I'm free.'

'Free to act like any other beastly skunk who tires of a woman overnight! Well, you don't get away with it as easily as that. Not if I know it! This is between you and me. If you mean to fight us you may as well know what you're up against.'

The words showed clearly her intention — an intention which the crowd read with a morbid pleasure and expectancy. Some of the spectators were eyeing the constable critically, fearing that he would intervene. He had moved close to the monument, but now looked on as helplessly as the rest. Had the woman been anyone but Florrie he would have acted promptly to prevent a breach of the peace. But this was the inhuman, subterranean conflict, an eddy of the warring tides of Beale and Potter and this conflict was outside his sphere, outside civic law, deep in the elemental clay, the absolute. He watched tensely, finding relief from the intolerable frustration in visualizing this as another of Bert's encounters in the ring.

150

Bert himself realized the threat of imminent danger in Florrie's words. He drew back against the body of the cross: but not quickly enough. Florrie had leapt on to the step and, her face convulsed with an insane, animal ferocity, had struck Bert with all her strength, twice in rapid succession, in the face. The first blow was a stinging slap that was heard all over the Square, but the second was not given with the open palm but with the fingers curled almost to a fist, so that the long nails dug into Bert's flesh, tearing in it a gash from the mouth up towards the left eye.

Having struck, she stood before him, crouching slightly and with her hands clenched, panting and quivering in anticipation of the final deadly clash, the violent draining out of the deeps of their old sensual passion, the last sadistic ecstacy that would release them from the personal tensions of intimacy.

But Bert was already released; there was nothing in him to be drained out. He was filled with a quality of life unknown to her. She, and the crowd that waited breathlessly, expecting her to stagger back at the next instant under a blow from the boxer's fist, were disappointed. Bert's face became dark and ugly, his arm jerked up — but it was not to strike. He pulled a red handkerchief from his pocket and wiped the blood from his cheek. After a minute he rallied, his eyes groping out to the crowd.

'That's all that Beale can do to me now,' he said quietly. The shadow passed from him as his glance lit on Rodda; his lips twitched with a wry, whimsical humour. 'And 'tisn't much after all: I'm used to having a bit o' blood let out.'

He turned back to Florrie as slowly she retreated down the steps, and sobered again at the sight of her flagging monstrous face.

'I'd bring you around too if I could,' he went on, 'and break Beale's grip from 'ee. But the bond is too close maybe. You're apart from the rest, moving among us with a mystery and meaning that only Beale and Potter know. I'm afraid 'tis no good hoping *you'll* ever go to Potter's Lane.'

She stiffened in a final despairing flash of rebellion.

'Potter's Lane!' she yelled back at him. 'I'd rather go to Helburn!'

'Aye: me and Tim heard something last night that explains why,' responded Bert, his voice tremulous as he peered at her, shrinking from the sense of palpable evil that flowed upon him from the wolfish figure.

'Tim's got more sense than you have,' she cried shrilly. '*He'd* never fall for Potter's damned tricks.'

She glanced across at Timothy, who had followed the tense scene with a fascinated relish, fear of the unknown spiritual undercurrents mingled with renascent desire for the impassioned form of the girl. He was magnetized by the flame in her, wishing to feel it break upon him in both its moods: the carnal heat searing his body, the insane hatred lashing at his brain, rousing him to the conflict which Bert denied her.

The appeal of her hunger was irresistible as her eyes met his. He lurched a few steps towards her, dazedly. But she was not ripe for him, here in public, weakened and humiliated by her encounter with Bert. A white mask of emotional exhaustion crept up over her face, dulling the eyes, drawing the lips taut over the teeth. She turned from him and hurried past the still groups, moving brokenly under their concentrated gaze until she disappeared around the corner.

As soon as she was gone Rodda tried to dissolve the uncanny spell by exercising his normal authority. He

152

motioned to Bert with a stiff, official gesture of command.

'That'll do, Truscott. This has gone far enough. You'd better quit.'

Bert nodded, stepping awkwardly down from the monument and taking in familiar details in an attempt to stand firmly amid commonplaces.

'This isn't your fight,' he said, addressing the constable. 'But it shows that lot at the manor is on the run. Potter'll have 'em out yet, and you may as well be on the winning side — all of 'ee.'

Amid a strained silence Bert strolled northward through the Square. He still held the handkerchief, and dabbed at the bleeding wound several times, but with the stolid unconcern of a practised boxer.

Before he had passed from view Mrs Rickard broke the hush, striking her window frame with a resounding thump as she looked incredulously at Mrs Tabb.

'Well, I never!' she exclaimed. 'I wouldn't ha' believed it if I hadn't seen it with me own eyes. He was right in one point: 'tisn't Bert Truscott we've seen here this morning. If 'twas Bert there'd have been a ambulance sent for by this time to take Florrie to hospital — or what was left of her.'

'I don't call him a man at all, to take they slaps lying down,' said Mrs Tabb sourly. 'He've lost all his guts in that lane, like any other man would.'

'No other man have been there in living memory,' replied Mrs Rickard.

Mrs Tabb appeared to be deliberating, casting about for some broader and less disquieting aspect of the problem.

'I aren't so sure,' she observed at length, peering reminiscently southward over the beacon. 'I mind some such doings years ago, one time while Parson Bully was laid up with inflammation. There was William Grose, what went out to South Africa. He was said to go in Potter's Lane, and it made a changed man of him all right.'

Mrs Rickard stepped back to her bed for a duster, which she proceeded to shake out of the window.

'Maybe so; but he was very reserved about it,' she remarked. 'None o' your bawling and shouting like Mrs Yelland and Bert.'

'The sight was similar, Mrs Rickard, but the nature was different. A very quiet man was William: well do I mind him, poor chap, a bite with a snake in Africa and dead and buried before he knowed what was happening. 'Twas a surprising end to a good man.'

'Mysteries will happen,' said Mrs Rickard, eyeing the corner around which Bert had disappeared.

'So they will.' Mrs Tabb spoke impressively, aware that the groups in the street were following the dialogue with growing interest. 'William was such a strapping chap, too. I can see him now as he used to walk through the Square here with bits o' paper stuck around his face where he'd cut hisself while shaving.'

'He was a most peculiar man in that respect,' commented Mrs Rickard, fingering her own chin and cheeks nervously. 'I can't mind seeing him outdoors without his face plastered up wi' paper to stop the blood flowing. A brave tender skin he must have had.'

'A soft, mild man all over William was: too mild for the maids, for none of 'em here to Carn Veor ever took on with him.'

Mrs Rickard dropped her duster on to the bedroom floor.

'Ellen Pascoe was said to be very sweet on him after he left,' she remarked tentatively.

'Yes, after he left,' repeated Mrs Tabb with a little grunt of derision. 'Just like Ellen's luck, not to know she was in love with a man till he'd gone ten thousand miles away and a snake had bite'n into his coffin. He never guessed her tender feelings, and the man died a bachelor.'

'And Bert will do the same, mark my words,' announced Mrs Rickard prophetically. 'Potter's Lane is no safe place for a single man, and seeing what've happened to Bert I'm glad our Harry's finishing his work to Potter's farm.'

Mrs Tabb reached up to adjust casually the rings of her curtain pole.

'I've never been able to understand,' she said, 'how your Harry was fool enough to work for Potter at all. We'd nearly forgot the fellow by that time: nobody here was saying he wanted workers.'

'You know Harry was given a trial because Potter heard he'd been in the lane,' replied Mrs Rickard grudgingly. 'Harry'd heard the lane cracked up as the best place in the district for soothing the nerves; a travelling cheapjack was telling people so at an open-air meeting in St Petroc — one of Potter's agents in disguise, I suppose. It caught Harry in a weak mood when he was willing to do things he'd have laughed at in his normal state.'

'We all guessed where the mood came from,' observed Mrs Tabb. 'There was signs of Harry staying a bachelor before he went to Potter's Lane. He had a nasty scat last Easter.'

Mrs Rickard cleared her throat, addressing her reply to the crowd below rather than to Mrs Tabb.

'That was idle gossip, without the slightest foundation,' she insisted, her eyes flashing angrily. 'Harry was shocked, as we all were, when Elsie Spry came to such a

155

terrible end, but he never had a serious thought about the girl.'

'He'd been seen talking to her,' Mrs Tabb retorted.

'It meant nothing whatever. The girl never darkened our doors.'

'Well, as Harry wasn't an invalid like Joe Gool you'd hardly expect her to, at that stage. 'Twas the next carnival queen who started they bold antics here. But everyone could see Harry was fair stunned over Elsie hanging herself — and he went to Potter's Lane just afterwards.'

'He may have gone to the lane,' declared Mrs Rickard in a tone of finality, 'but he can't be classed with these others. He wasn't so silly as Bert, to go on when it got dark and rough, tearing his Sunday-best trousers. He only ventured a few yards in and never saw anything but thorns and stinging nettles.'

Part Three
The Slain

Apart from the final word of forgiveness, erotic passions are as precarious as the passions of politics; their vigorous energy can — apart from the final word 'Resurrection' — produce only fruit unto death.

Karl Barth

Chapter Fifteen

BRONWEN stood limply in the doorway of her home, watching her father disappear around the corner. It was now past noon, the Square was silent and empty but for the birds. She looked about it restlessly, her face pale, twitching. She leaned against the door jamb and clenched her hands.

Though Bronwen stood still her spirit was in flight. All day she had been pursued, hag-ridden from the moment her mind pulled sluggishly up the black slime of nightmare which had sucked exhaustingly at her brain during her few hours of sleep.

It was nine o'clock when she awoke. The first sounds she heard were the voices of people in the Square, and before she had dressed, while she stood quite naked in front of the wardrobe and took up a garment from the bed, she heard the name she most hated. The groups outside were discussing Bert's conversion, and the tremendous increase of Potter's power that would result from it.

Bronwen had been naked when she heard Potter's name spoken, and ever since it had been stripping her soul, probing along the clay strata, the carnal veins, unblemished and intact in their virtue yet alien to Potter, and ineffectual, for the thought of him tore out the roots of every comforting illusion, layer by layer, down to the raw bedrock of instinct.

Timothy was in the back garden when she came downstairs. He had important matters to decide, and wished to be alone and to say nothing until he had resolved on his new course amid the rapidly changing circumstances.

159

Bronwen did not call him in, or take anything of the rough breakfast he had prepared. She felt unable to stay in the house, hemmed in by the excited groups whose continual talk of Potter smote in through the window and stung her. She hurried outdoors, hatless and wearing her pinafore that was torn and dirty, and passed through the Square, speaking to none of the neighbours who greeted her. Her mind was tautened, closed rigidly against the name of Potter. She hastened towards the Gummas' cottage.

There, no doubt, she would find diversion, escape from the bitter drama that lay nearer home. There were Mrs Prynne's feet to be talked of, and the fowls to be seen, and Maggie might be about to have her baby. It would be a relief to gossip on these neutral matters, emerging from the stifling rut of conflict to the broad, sane levels of everyday life.

But she had been forestalled; here again the cunning of Potter had outwitted her plan. She had been greeted at the Gummas' door by Maggie — but not the Maggie she had expected to find, the gross, peevish creature she had seen at Budge's shop yesterday. Maggie was smiling, and Bronwen felt in her at once the same atmosphere as that which pervaded the groups in the Square: she was allied with Mrs Yelland under some powerful hypnotic influence. And to Bronwen the transformation was a rebuke: Maggie was now superior to her, illuminated. Until now there had been nothing sublime or even dignified about Maggie's condition. She was a mere human substance on which Nature had played an obscene trick — pitiful, yet scarcely inspiring compassion in the beholder, so stolidly and brutishly did she submit to the outrage. It could even be thought that when her child was born she would hardly suffer. Nature would suffer a brief pang through the dense and uncomprehending substance as she pressed another clot into the dull clay-lands; but as an individual, a person with separate longings, apprehensions and achievements, she would not participate in the reality of the creative process. She was not sufficiently alert or aware, not sensitive, so completely had the pettiness of her spirit blunted and deadened her body. But now there was something awesome in the heavy fecundity of the flesh; it was freed from the burden of a paltry mind, from the shadow of Maggie's old fear and hatred of Potter.

Maggie laid a hand on Bronwen's arm with a new, eager friendliness.

'I'm glad you've come,' she said fervently. 'I've been thinking of our talk in the shop — the trouble about Joe — and I'm longing to tell 'ee what's happened.'

Bronwen stared, biting her lip as dully the realization seeped through and Potter's name was clanged afresh, maddeningly.

Mrs Prynne came hobbling from the kitchen, carrying a broom, which she pointed gleefully at her daughter. She was a large, flabby old woman with a blotchy simpering face and a very soft, sly voice.

'I never thought decent folks like we would ever owe anything to Rosa Nance,' she chuckled. 'But we'm all singing the praise o' that little harlot this morning. She used to bewitch the men, but 'tis a good spell she cast on Maggie — she and Potter between 'em . . .'

Bronwen had shaken off Maggie's hand and was hurrying down to the gate, her head bent, the nails of her clenched fingers dug into her palms. Something within her was ripping like that, cruelly, unveiling the monstrous images: Beale's hands, and a dead horse, blood in the well. Maggie had not seen the well or the horse, only the Rock, Potter's Rock . . .

161

Bronwen slunk back home like a desperate, hunted animal. She admitted her bafflement, the impossibility of escape, and had no defence but the frantic clawing of her trapped selfhood. She expected further pressure that would crush even this resistance and was numbly acquiescent when, as she turned into the Square, she saw the stocky bow-legged figure of George Gumma halt outside her home and speak to her father, who was standing at the gate, frowning perplexedly. She supposed he had just discovered that she was not in the house.

Slowly she approached the two men, shrinking, for she knew George was about to tell her father of his and Maggie's experience in Potter's Lane. When she came within a few yards of the gate George glanced around at her and lifted his trilby. He was a very excitable man, but his present excitement was agreeable and made his rough gipsy-like face attractive.

'You been over paying missus a call, eh?' he enquired.

'Only for a minute,' she replied, hard and tight-lipped.

'You noticed the change, I bet. I been paying a call meself — up to Nances'. Had a bit of apologizing to do.' He jerked his arm at Timothy. 'Heard any noise here last night, about ten o'clock?'

'No, I never,' grunted Timothy, staring fixedly at Bronwen.

'I thought I heard a scream,' remarked the girl, anxious to prolong this digression until she was safely indoors, 'and I sat up in bed, listening to hear it again. But I reckoned 'twas my nerves: I was upset last evening.'

'The scream was real enough, Bron, and it happened like this.' George leaned against the gate-post, and as

162

Timothy was already propped against the other Bronwen could not pass. 'Maggie came home last night saying Rosa'd took her to Potter's Lane and she's seen the Rock and everything was all right. I was so shocked I had to work off me spleen somehow, so I went out meaning to get a stick o' dynamite from Beale's works and blow the Rock to pieces. Out here to corner I overtook Rosa and she tried to stop me going on. But I wasn't in any mood to listen to her, and when she grabbed me arm I gave her a flip or two in the face to make her let go. But I'm glad she didn't stop me — and so was she when she heard how it turned out. I seen Bert Truscott too and we all feel we've set the ball rolling. Your motive don't matter — the Rock gets you if you see it.'

Timothy folded his arms and nodded smartly at the war memorial, around which several children were playing — the only persons now in the Square. The women had gone indoors to attend to their cooking.

'Wonders will never cease in this world,' observed Timothy; 'but a wonder isn't no credit when it d'mean that you'm a fool.'

Bronwen's lip curled; her eyes flashed at George — deliberate, scornful.

'You and Mag is near as stodgy as the Yellands,' she said, her voice struggling to convey a vague grossness. 'A rock may be good enough to thrill you. But I don't fancy it: I've had better things, see?'

'So you have,' Timothy agreed, jerking a thumb at her approvingly. 'But if you want more of it,' he added, his manner hardening as she squeezed past him, 'you'd better get Joe Gool out o' your mind. He never come here last night, and 'tis my opinion he won't darken these doors again. And 'tis no good 'ee going over to Gools': they'd think you was pestering the chap now there's no chance of'n marrying 'ee . . .'

163

When George was gone and Bronwen had rolled pastry for a pie, Timothy told her the decision he had reached through his brooding in the garden.

'Things is worked around for me after all,' he said, slipping off the floury table and smacking with both hands the seat of his trousers. 'There was a bit of a hitch last evening, and I spoke words that must be took back.'

'About — marrying Florrie?'

'That's it. I saw meanings in her eyes when she looked at me this morning after giving Bert that stinger, and I'm minded to nip in while she's keen. I believe I could bring her around to make a wedding of it. The maid have got a hold on me somehow, and I can't help meself if she's willing.'

Bronwen moved to the stove, peering hard at him.

''Tis through Beale, I feel that,' she said, shuddering. 'While you're in thick with him you can't resist her, even when you see what a devil she can be in some of her moods. You held out against Rosa — but this is different.'

'Aye: there's reasons I could tell if I liked.' Timothy spoke in a somewhat hesitant tone, his eyes evasive, downcast. 'It did shake me when I heard Beale's tale last night, but I don't mind now more'n Bert did. 'Tis Florrie herself I'm itching for, wherever she came from.'

Bronwen turned wearily, confused between the spiritual and material threats.

'Well, you must please yourself, dad. I didn't know whether you might — follow the others now — Bert and Rosa and they Gummas — and get free o' Beale too.'

Timothy shook his head decidedly.

'I'm sound at the top yet, I hope,' he muttered. 'I warned Bert 'twasn't safe for any man's brains to see the insides o' Potter's Lane — and I was right.

164

We'll be a village o' lunatics if this d'go much further. But I'll stand my ground to the last. And you will, too, I believe?'

'Of course. It's terrible to see how they're all caving in, thinking Potter really cares for 'em. I wish they knew as much as me and Joe do!' The bitter flash spent itself, she was clouded again, seeking support. 'I'm glad I can depend on you, dad . . . But I wish you could hold out going so far in the other camp.'

'I aren't thinking of any camp at all,' retorted Timothy. 'I'm after Florrie to please meself, not Beale.'

'But to think of you living there with him like Balker did! . . . I don't believe I could screw up enough courage to go in that house, even if Florrie'd let me.'

Bronwen turned her back to Timothy, trying with the aid of the poker to open a stubborn flue. The heat of the stove brought sweat to her face, but a feverish dread was also upon it when she next spoke.

'Don't you feel scared, dad, o' living with Beale now everything's going against him? Haven't you thought — something awful might happen soon, from Beale's side, to try and stop the wave that's sweeping one after another down to Potter's Lane?'

Timothy shrugged uneasily, his face dark and tense with the memory of the inhuman desperation he had observed in Beale last night.

'The man'll be pretty mad about it, no doubt o' that,' he said. 'But I don't reckon he'll tackle the job from this side the river. More likely he'll clear out for a time, as he did before Florrie was born, and plan a big move from Helburn. That'd leave me and Florrie free there at the manor.'

'But I . . . what *shall* I do, dad?'

There was panic in her voice, but Timothy's response was gruffly practical.

'Got your own life to live, haven't 'ee? You can't go hanging round your father all your days. And you only got yourself to blame for taking up wi' such a little runt as Joe. If 'twas any other chap you could ha' married this summer. And if you'm so scared o' Beale having his vengeance and wiping us all out, you needn't wait long, even as 'tis. They lips could be kissed this very night if you'd go out around and whistle to the first chap you fancy. I know how some of 'em d'look at 'ee; they wouldn't need to be asked twice.'

Bronwen shivered now, recalling these scenes; she stepped out into the Square and glanced up and down the road and into the sky. She saw and heard nothing that could communicate with her. Life around her was rich, relaxed, colourful with vivid splashes of flowers behind garden gates, butterflies and bees nosing through the lower drifts and eddies of pale sunshine, birds swooping in the unbroken light overhead . . . But she was bruised and stiffened, aching impotently for release.

As a natural creature she wished to feel the mystery of blood and soil, the fecundity. She wished to feel the wave flow unchecked within and about her, finding her body as congruous as the flower stems, drawing it into the orbit in which the seed of plant and bird and beast and man were quickened alike, born to the earth-mother and the sun. But she was aware that there was something else, a force that threatened this unity — much as the aura of sanctity in a church threatened it, but more powerfully. Although she was only dimly conscious of this disruptive force, the faintest shadow of it, even the hint she had felt in Maggie that morning, was terrifying to her — as terrifying as the power of Beale's hands from which she had fled, though entirely different in essence.

166

She sensed this force as a reversal of the normal concept of the seasons, for where its impact was felt winter became the truly creative season, the season of stark surrender: the bare rock, the stripped tree were symbols of eternal energy that derided the transient efflorescence of spring. This too could be apprehended amid the cold enclosure of a church; but why should it be linked with Potter's Lane? Why did she feel it only because of the experience that had come to Mrs Yelland and Maggie? She herself had never been inside Carn Veor church, but she knew that its recent priests had been hostile to Potter, and this deepened the mystery. The ecclesiastical gloom was akin to that of the lane between the marshes, yet the influence of the Rock could be regarded only as an intrusion here under the shadow of the church. It was not evil like the power of Beale, but it seemed equally offensive.

In her present state, raw with the sting of personal rebuff, Bronwen loathed it, retreating upon the barren selfhood, realizing that there too Potter had struck home. The sundering and transmuting element was released by the person who had refused to employ Joe and thus, by another mood than that of the Rock, had cast her back from the spring wave, piercing and breaking up the very sunbeams that flowed against her bare flesh. She felt herself abandoned, debarred from the neutral ground of earthly fulfilment, forced upon the darkened uplands of conflict where she was menaced from both sides, torn with her old dread of the power of Beale, cowering in dumb, impotent hatred before the onset of Potter's assault.

Bronwen was in despair, but she resisted the obvious temptation that Timothy had urged, the release through a headlong flight to another young man. Joe was so unlike anyone else in the village that her whole conception of love, her whole approach to it, would have to be altered before she could be fit for a new mate. She had taken the peculiar nuances of Joe's nature — his moodiness, his sincerity, his odd, innocent clownishness: qualities so congenial to her that she could not bear to unlearn them through the impact of a more balanced, normal personality. The fact that their courtship had begun through childish love-play in a bedroom was also a deterrent: how was she to adjust herself to the common customs, the vulgar joking with youths at street corners? Such an atmosphere was like that of another world, a gross, tawdry world, compared with the sheltered, glowing domesticity of the ripening she had known with Joe; bending over the bed for their first kiss, quickening with his moods as he grew stronger until they could snuggle together on the sofa downstairs. She could not get back to that again elsewhere; it was a dead past unless she married Joe. And nothing but the fulfilment of that separate way would satisfy her. She knew it, and the knowledge was agony, sharpened by the pressure Timothy had now exerted by his decision to marry and leave her to fend for herself. And that too was a stroke of Potter's, reaching her through Bert Truscott.

The sense of malicious fate hemming her in completely, mocking her, was so strong that she accepted as a fitting climax of irony the shock through her nerves when, probing mutinously the upper end of the Square, she saw Joe himself slouching around the corner. And she realized at once, as he waved to her, that a strange reversal had taken place. Joe had completely lost the weariness which Mr Reed had noted in him as he pushed his barrow towards the clay-dump a few hours earlier, but his fresh vitality was unnatural; he seemed to have been galvanized into mechanical life. He was no longer crushed and benumbed, but he was still in rebellion. She shrank from him, shaken and bruised by the new wave of possibility. Suspense and incredulity gripped her until, in a sudden snapping of tension, she turned and fled back into the house. She closed the door and stood panting and stark-eyed, watching the window.

Joe drew nearer and had soon unlatched the gate; his shoes crunched the path, he opened the door without a rap and came in.

Bronwen was leaning against the table; she did not move. Her face was like an olive mask, the lips taut, the narrow forehead wrinkled, almost hidden by the tumbling gingery wisps of her hair.

'Joe!' she murmured in reproach and perplexity. 'Why've you come here now? Did father call?'

Joe halted by the partition and grinned at her. The jollity that had been smothered in him yesterday at Priory Bridge had rekindled, but there was something artificial and repulsive about it. His lean face was flushed, the eyes glowing feverishly.

'Yes,' he replied; 'the old man came in like a thunder-cloud. We was having dinner — Gregory and his girl there too — but he didn't mind the visitors. Just wanted to lay down the law. Everything was over between us and I must leave the field free for some fellow who could give you a home this year.'

'I knew he'd warn you off,' she said, still isolated from his mood. 'It's no good pretending, Joe. We're beat. It's been a terrible knock — on top of Potter's — to find what Florrie had up her sleeve when I saw her in the shop yesterday. If dad wasn't after her we could have waited, but now — you can *see* there's no future for us. I can't stop him marrying.'

Joe hung his cap on the stair-post and blinked up at an open bedroom door. He was still grinning.

169

'We can do something better than stopping your dad,' he said.

'How?'

'We can get married ourselves.'

Bronwen stepped out into the centre of the room, her mind pulling through eddies of faintness that left the tall figure a limp, flagging thing, drained of volition.

'Get married?' she repeated dazedly. 'Why — have you heard — anything more from Potter?'

Joe shook his head contemptuously; he kicked the bottom stair.

'That bloke! No, you wouldn't catch him turning generous. 'Tis somebody else — someone more important — who'll get us out o' this mess.'

The implication grew clearer, but she could not accept it. She continued to stare at him, pitiful in her bewilderment.

'Did you — tell dad?' she faltered.

'You bet I did!'

'What did he say about it?'

'Greased him down fine — you should have seen his face! He thought I was bluffing at first, but I told him he could ask when he got to the manor if he didn't believe me. He gave us his blessing before he went out, and advised me to come here straight away. I left the others greasing themselves on the fowl — though this turn have spoilt Gregory's appetite, I fancy.' Joe laughed with a hollow, boisterous malice.

'Poor old Greg — it took the wind out of his sails when he heard the news I had for him. He'd come to Carn Veor today expecting to do all the brag himself: going to college soon to study for school-teaching — everything opening out for him to marry his fine town girl. He thought to find me a helpless invalid who'd just have to listen and say nothing but congratulations. And instead — I could tell him I was courting too and — and starting work tomorrow.'

'But where, Joe — where? What's happened? Tell me.' She seemed to be calling to him across a widening gulf. She felt the urge to go to him and seize his arm. But she remained by the table, only her eyes groping for contact.

Joe sensed the danger and became uneasily aggressive as he resumed:

'It's all linked up with Gregory's visit. I went over to the burrow for a load of sand this morning, to smarten up our path a bit. 'Twas hardly fit for visitors to see — plastered with earth after so much gardening lately, and I wasn't in the mood to fetch it last night. While I was loading up — Beale arrived in his car, came to see how much damage was done to the engine-house. Florrie was with him, but she couldn't have stayed long on the claywork: she soon went down to the Square and let fly at Bert. But when he saw me with the barrow he stopped and waited till I caught up with him and — and asked me if I'd like a job: helping to clean up the mess around the engine-house and then fetching sand for making cement to rebuild it. So Balker clearing out have proved lucky for our family, giving your father the woman he wants and opening the way for me to get the girl I want. Everything's OK after all, and I could give three cheers over the wish-bone as I said I would yesterday — but not for old Potter.'

Bronwen stood inert, watching his lips — the lips of a mature man, babbling childishly. It was strange, he was trying to communicate something to her. Something about Beale and the gutted engine-house. She was fascinated as by a chance contact with insanity, merely a witness, unimplicated.

Joe lurched towards her, scanning her warily, as if

171

measuring his strength against hers. His manner was gloating and unwholesome, with a latent brutality.

'I told your dad it might take some pretty hectic love-making to bring you around to this,' he said in a thick tense tone. 'So I'd better make a start now, eh?'

He wanted to see her face rouse from the blank mask, become alive with that hard yet tender potency which had been her peculiar lure for him. But there was deadly fear upon the dark unaltering mask, the fixed grey eyes were unknown to him, burnt out, distant. She had drawn back upon the table, one of her big hands clawing the air vaguely to ward him off, the other covering her face, the gaunt knotty fingers stifling a cry:

'No — don't touch me!'

It was the first time she had repulsed him and Joe stood rigid, baffled and incredulous as the horror closed upon him.

Chapter Sixteen

BERT TRUSCOTT had never thought of marrying. He had decided early in life that he was not the sort of man who could make a success of marriage. His physical tastes were erratic and no one woman could ever have satisfied him for more than a few weeks. He seemed to have been born with an emotional nature in a state of disintegration, for he could not remember the time when he had felt differently. The process had not begun through his abandonment of moral restraints; it was rather that, being so constituted, he had instinctively rejected moral restraint as odious and alien to him. His sense of touch was particularly keen, and his reactions were violent and unpredictable. Sometimes he could only be stimulated by girls who were plump. At other times he could be repelled by all plump women and could be roused only by thin ones. He had never tried to conquer this idiosyncrasy: it was essential that he should retain it in order to be Bert Truscott. And it was not a problem on which the moralist could make any relevant comment; it was entirely physical and involuntary.

The platitudes of the Carn Veor vicarage could not cut deep enough to reach Bert's predicament. They could not get into his blood and nerves and turn back the currents of heredity that had given him this broken and spasmodic appetite. But gradually, throughout this Sunday morning, he realized that the incredible thing had happened: the power of the Rock had penetrated and was working back through these channels, cleansing and steadying all the springs of impulse within him. It was not merely that his spiritual life was quickened

173

and his mental outlook adjusted: he was aware of a new potentiality in the drive of instinct along his nerves — a discipline that stilled the false, darting movements. And as his desire narrowed to its true channel it broke with overwhelming force towards Rosa. When he learnt from George Gumma that Rosa also had been through Potter's Lane he knew that she was destined for him in the will of Potter.

Early in the afternoon he left his home, wearing his best navy-blue suit and grey cap, and strolled towards the Nances' home, his big, raw-boned face looking unusually sober and expectant. The village was now quiet, but the moorland clayworks were noisy with the slur of wagons and the puffing of engines in the winder-houses — brittle and obscene challenges to Bert's mood, reminding him of the gross activities in which he had taken part in those regions, of the malignant powers that were still being generated there — powers he would have to combat till Potter again ruled Carn Veor. But his mood carried him over these threats towards the ful-filment and solace which he knew awaited him in Rosa's cottage.

On reaching it he wondered whether the Nances were abed, for no sound came from within the house, but he strode resolutely up the path, making a good deal of noise to warn them of his approach. Having arrived at the doorstep he was almost knocked backward as Mrs Nance suddenly emerged — a short woman, ugly and bald — carrying a bowl of greasy water. She stared at Bert through her steel-rimmed spectacles, expressing a good-humoured contempt.

'All right, Bert,' she mumbled, passing on towards the drain at the house corner. 'I aren't much sur-prised . . .'

Bert entered the house very quietly, cap in hand, and

174

found Rosa sitting alone on the parlour sofa. She was combing her hair that lay in thick golden coils over her breasts and shoulders. Bert knew at a glance that he had not been deceived: her face, lifting like a pale bruised petal, grew radiant, the big blue eyes searching and accepting him as frankly as in the past, but with a different motive, a strange primitive purity resembling that of a priestess.

As he came in she rose, her soft flamy beauty cutting upon the sour dead scene visible through the window. In the foreground was the sullen church tower, and behind it, tiny at the foot of the slope, the blackened shell of the engine-house, the jagged roofless walls looming coarsely against the white sand. Rosa had now turned her back on that squalid symbol, yet Bert felt confused recalling their brief encounter in the Square yesterday while the ruins were still smouldering. The flicker of intimate memories disturbed him. He had so often used her with a cheap, random mastery, he was mortified; but he could scarcely ask her forgiveness, for until now her beauty had been in itself a poisonous thing, a rank lotus blossoming at night in the pit-slime. The change in them both was so profound it made him inarticulate, and he attempted a joke.

'I had to come in to see how the invalid's getting on,' he greeted.

Rosa smiled, playfulness veiling the deeps in her also.

'Oh, there's a good chance of recovery, I believe,' she said lightly. 'It's only a bruise or two. D'you know George has been here?'

'Aye; and if I hadn't seen Potter's Rock meself 'tis he who'd be a invalid!'

'It was my own fault,' she answered, sobering as she resumed her seat and dropped the comb beside her. 'We

175

all know what George is like in a temper. Only I was afraid . . .'

She studied Bert's face, which was marked by several scratches — most of them faint, relics of his boxing bouts during recent months, but one on the left cheek was fresh and looked as if it had only just stopped bleeding. She understood suddenly and her eyes narrowed, hardening for a moment.

'We've both got something to show for going into Potter's Lane last night,' she commented.

Bert too flinched under the renewed sense of defilement, but he met her gaze steadily.

'You've heard — about Florrie?'

'Yes. It's gone all around the village. You showed great restraint, Bert.'

'Well, I deserve what she gave me when you look at it from her standpoint. Only last night out to Beale's I promised her . . . But let's forget it. 'Tisn't healthy to think of, they things isn't.'

'You aren't afraid of — of anything further happening?'

'No. Beale hisself can't touch me, and I don't think Florrie'll try again.'

Bert stepped across to the sofa, ducking beneath the hanging brass lamp, and sat down. He put an arm around Rosa's waist, rather shyly, as if this were the first time he had touched her. Rosa smiled, sharing his sense of freshness, of unusedness, the feeling of having all to learn yet about this art of love in which she had thought herself so expert for nearly ten years.

Mrs Nance again entered the house. They heard her deposit the bowl with a clatter in the 'spence' and then ascend the stairs to the bedroom where her husband had been confined for several months with a spinal affliction. Mrs Nance always went upstairs when a man

176

called to see Rosa — which was seldom, for there was a peculiar harsh realism in Rosa's way of life that was not suited to the daintiness, the voluptuousness of a bed indoors. She had been a harlot of the rocks and the clay, the stripped, almost masochistic region of sensuality.

Bert and Rosa were content for a while to muse upon the strange experience that had come to them, to sit with their arms around each other, their free hands clasped in Rosa's lap and glance about the room, familiar yet subtly changed, subdued and congruous to the new mood in them.

The. parlour was snug, low-ceilinged, rather stuffy now, for sunlight and kindling fire combined to warm it. A worm-eaten harmonium faced the sofa, and an armchair with broken springs stood beside it, one of its legs inside the fender. In the corner beyond the doorway was a glass-fronted cabinet, its three shelves laden with china souvenirs, tiny granite crosses, specimens of lead and copper ore, and dainty cups and saucers that, being cracked or broken, were unfit even for display.

It was at these that Bert was staring meditatively when he next spoke.

''Tis wonderful what's happening here in Carn Veor,' he remarked. 'George was telling me what a difference there is already in Gummas' place. George came home from Potter's Lane and went right across to Maggie as she stood by the kitchen table, and kissed her; and there they are living like a honeymoon couple, and both looking forward to see whether what's coming is boy or maid. No fear at all in Maggie now, so George said; and he've vowed he'll be a good husband to her from now on. As soon as he saw the Rock, he said, it went through him like a knife, what a brute he'd been to Maggie. He forgot all about the dynamite.'

177

'Yes, he was bound to; I needn't have interfered really,' murmured Rosa, turning to draw aside the green curtain behind the couch. She looked broodingly out of the window, across at the Church, about which rooks were flying, and at the yew tree by the cemetery gate. She remembered how she had found Maggie there and led her away from the dull clammy corruption, into the healing shade of Potter's Lane.

Bert edged back a little, and as his eyes took the full sweep of her figure — she wore a blue short-sleeved frock — the certainty of the miracle deepened within him. The old horrible instability of appetite was gone — not because his appetite was now focussed on Rosa, but because he was beyond appetite. Though her body pulled upon him with a new magnetism, he was fused with her at a deeper level than the flesh could feed on. The sense of power was charged with a fear of trespass, liberating the soul.

'I didn't mean to go in the lane till yesterday,' Rosa continued; 'though it's been a hard fight for years, with nobody guessing . . . It wasn't a sudden impulse with me. I heard when — when I was twelve that I should get free o' Beale one day. "He won't always be in the way," I was told. I've always minded they words.'

'Who was it told 'em to 'ee?' enquired Bert.

'I can't be sure, but I think it must have been Potter's servant.'

Bert stared in bewilderment.

'Where did 'ee see she to?' he asked.

'In the lane.'

'What lane?'

'I — I've been there before,' faltered Rosa.

'Not in Potter's, where you went last night?' For a moment Bert felt a sickening flurry of insecurity that brought a darkness and tenseness to his face.

'Yes. I went there when I was twelve,' admitted Rosa.

'But you didn't see . . .?'

'No, I didn't see the Rock — didn't think of it. That was why it — it got messed up. But I did feel *some* things as soon as the shade of the thorn trees touched me. Things about love . . . I can hardly explain, even to you . . .'

'I've felt 'em meself now,' said Bert. 'But you — you was turned back somehow?'

'I was . . . But I'd better not tell you about that.'

Bert looked closely at her, then drew a quick breath. He understood: he too had felt the incubus, and on the spirit of a girl of twelve it would have been over-whelming, the grossness of menace.

'I can guess,' he said grimly, 'if — if you mean Beale was in the lane.'

Rosa assented by a slow nod of her head, shuddering.

Bert's hands clenched, his face was taut and ugly until she showed him in her caresses how truly they were beyond being *touched* by that now.

'And then,' continued Rosa, 'as soon as Beale was gone I found this woman there — Potter's servant, I'm sure. She told me not to cry or let anyone know what had happened, for 'twouldn't matter when I grew up and understood. And now I do . . .' She drew Bert's face to hers, kissing tenderly the scar which Florrie had left on his cheek.

''Twas you I really wanted, Bert, even then, I believe. I've never forgot how it came to me, the longing to find a chap in the lane. That may have been the wrong turn that Beale took advantage of, but there was some hint o' Potter's blessing in it. You must have been nearly twenty then. If only I'd met you instead o' Beale! I wonder what would have happened?'

179

Bert smiled whimsically across at the fire, but he spoke soberly.

'If we'd gone on together to see the Rock there'd ha' been a miracle,' he replied. 'Maybe we'd have minded Potter's by-law and knelt in the ruined shrine where Bully's tree crashed down. We'd have known what was in store for us and had patience.'

'Yes — oh, it *would* have been different — all along. Potter's been waiting all these years for us to take the step we took last evening.'

'I believe he has,' agreed Bert. 'And Beale haven't stopped us getting there in the end. Neither he, nor Florrie, nor Smithers and they claywork men — nor the maids who liked to see me stripped in the ring. None of 'em haven't stopped Potter's plan. All we've done under Beale's shadow is gone from us now like our old clothes. And what's left — what's *come* to us, Rosa — that's for each other, every bit of it, and always.'

Silence fell between them until the church clock boomed the half hour after one. Somebody was heard approaching the pump outside, then came the rhythmic creak of the handle, the splash of water and Miss Pascoe's voice, mumbling agitatedly. When she had gone into her home with the filled pitcher, Rosa showed that the distraction had given her thoughts a new slant.

'I wonder what's wrong with Miss Pascoe?' she observed, a perplexed frown sobering her face. 'She's out of step with the rest of us. I saw her last night while I was out here with Maggie, and asked her if she'd been to Potter's Lane, but she didn't speak. I can't make her out at all.'

Bert pondered for a few moments, his hand on Rosa's shoulder.

'Ellen always lived apart from our hot ways here in Carn Veor,' he said presently. 'She can't put the power o' the Rock into practice straight off like we others. Mrs Yelland came home to her man, Maggie came home to George — and now I've come to you. But Ellen had to come home to a empty house — nobody to share her feelings with, so they're bottled up, I s'pose.'

There was an undertone in Bert's voice that made Rosa thrill with joy and assurance. He had no need to propose marriage; the consummation was implied and accepted, beyond conventional formula, deep within the illumination of real values. Her eyes softened as they met his, and she spoke with freshening intensity.

'I can't think what the Rock can mean to a woman like Miss Pascoe. A middle-aged spinster — never even been kissed so far as I know. I always felt Potter's Lane had special meaning for *that* side of life: I don't know why, unless it was the dark heavy trees — like going through a jungle — and the marshes outside with the water that made me think of baptism — religion and love mixed somehow. But it can't mean that for *everyone*: Potter wants all of us to be rid of Beale's grip, whether we marry or not. And I know now it isn't just human love . . . There were moments last night when I felt like a nun . . .'

She paused, listening intently as further sounds came from the adjoining cottage. A door banged and quick confused footsteps clattered down to the road. The pair on the sofa glanced curiously out and saw Miss Pascoe's lean distraught figure appear over the low shrubs that bordered the Nances' garden. Her uncovered greying hair blew around her bowed face. She passed within a few feet of Bert and Rosa, hurrying by the window to the kitchen door, and they heard her gabbling to herself:

'I must tell them — I must tell Mr Reed — in the very room — we'll have to take it up again in court — Rosa

181

and Mrs Yelland — we must all go and ask Mr Reed to take it up again. I shan't have a moment's rest till all the village knows it was me — me — and William dead in Africa only a month before!'

Chapter Seventeen

MR REED stood, talking with Beale, outside his church, the windows of which were dark. Above them the sky was only just becoming clouded, and the starlight cast a grey haze over the churchyard, illuminating the two dark-clad figures standing close together in the path beside a granite cross almost as tall as they.

Beale had come to Carn Veor this evening on a grimmer mission than any he had undertaken for many years. During the past twenty-four hours his losses had been catastrophic, beyond anything he had imagined yesterday when he returned from the gutted enginehouse. He had now left Florrie at home with Timothy, and as she had recklessly decided to marry him it was unlikely that he too would desert to Potter's side. But his influence would count for little against Bert's; the disaster was irreparable.

Beale had not slept at all last night, but had remained outdoors, pacing the grounds of the manor, crouching among the trees, visualizing Bert's unwitting approach to the Rock. He had thrown the whole force of his demonic energy hypnotically upon the lane, against the will of the boxer, against the election from beyond. But it was a futile resistance; the decree of Potter had broken him, the insatiable malice choosing its hour and its instruments. Learning from Florrie of Bert's confession in the Square and of Rosa's surrender, he had accepted defeat with an instinctive darting of his will to the plan he had made for this dire emergency. There was no escape from it now, no room for any reasoning or pity.

He too must choose his hour and his instrument at Helburn.

He could not make his counter-attack against any of the rebels. He knew that they were safe, that he could not touch them to bring harm upon them. Florrie's purely feminine outburst of violence against Bert was the limit to which, even indirectly, he could be revenged upon the boxer. Rosa he could not reach even through a man. That pair, and the others, were guarded by the Shadow, the power of the Rock.

On sighting the vicar standing forlornly in the church porch, Beale was goaded to a fierce malice and contempt. This, then, was his ally — this weak, shattered pathetic creature! The day had brought unrelieved misfortune to him also, and he obviously felt his humiliation in simple human terms. The vague hopes he had cherished as dawn broke over the clayworks had been ruthlessly mauled, his illusions pierced at the outset. Potter had forestalled him with such brutal mastery that his appeal for the sanity and dignity of a gradual reformation had not even been made. There had been no service in the church this evening, for no-one but the minister had come. Mrs Budge and Mr Teague had been the sole communicants this morning; Mr Teague alone, besides the bell-ringers, had appeared for the morning service. He had expected to find Miss Pascoe there and to observe the effect her experience in Potter's Lane might have upon her behaviour in church; but as neither she nor any other woman arrived, he had sniffed a little with his long nose and walked home again in a bad temper. Mr Reed had thus been routed even more completely than Beale himself.

Beale was lashed to a furious derision of this clerical wreck. But he was still acting a part; the mask was slipping, but it had not yet fallen. He could still control his reactions and, with the superficial part of his mind, evade the dark horror of the fixed resolve in the deeps of him. There was something here in the vicar's dereliction on which he could feed; it would not satisfy him, but the taste of a little real misery in a fellow creature would whet his appetite. He had stepped into the churchyard to offer the vicar his sympathy, speaking and acting from the surface of his mind, aware that he was soon to be unveiled and released, but that this was not the place or the moment.

Mr Reed was now expressing himself warmly in condemnation of the disgraceful conduct of the villagers who had allowed an immoral boxer to obstruct the due observance of religion in Carn Veor church. He was clearly bewildered by the occurrence, and strangely evasive about the deeper issues involved in it. He spoke as if Bert had launched the attack through mere personal enmity — the enmity of a brutal and profane man towards the forces of decency and virtue. He did not mention Potter or hint that Bert had become Potter's ally.

Beale read the vicar's mind; he fed upon the deadly fear of the Rock that bristled in the dark, furtive regions of Mr Reed's soul. This was something he also felt, something that relieved him of utter loneliness. It was his one comfort now, before the horror closed in for his retaliation, to see others sharing his impotence. After listening to the vicar's complaint he pondered for a few moments with bowed head, then laid a hand on Mr Reed's arm.

'I agree that the incident is a disgrace to the parish,' he replied in a tone that sounded icy and remote. 'But I warned you yesterday that the task confronting us is still formidable. Only slowly, in the teeth of Potter's opposition, can there be a broadening of the mental horizon

185

here, a removal of the anti-social prejudices, the distrust of outside influence, which have for so long shackled the inhabitants. A quiet, persistent effort will be needed before much impression is made on these stubborn and ignorant folk.'

'But it is necessary to establish contact with them,' protested Mr Reed irritably. 'And in the present temper of the village I doubt whether I could get a hearing even if I called at their homes. The situation seems almost out of hand, and the local police service, which could help to check the trouble, is far from efficient. I gather that the constable was present at the — er — disturbance. I think he should have stopped Truscott from fomenting these dangerous antagonisms — particularly on a Sunday morning.'

An ugly smile flickered across Beale's face in the darkness.

'My daughter was apparently more efficient than the constable in breaking up the meeting,' he observed, and there was a brief smouldering in his manner that caused Mr Reed to shrink from him. 'I'm not surprised that you are alarmed at the way things have developed since we talked in the office. You probably feel that the example of some of us at the manor is as bad as that of the villagers. But naturally I am not responsible for the conduct of my daughter and son-in-law. Florrie is a somewhat hysterical young woman — neurotic from birth. And you will realize her state of mind at being deserted by her husband.'

'Yes — yes, of course,' the vicar murmured confusedly.

'We have all struck a black patch,' resumed Beale. 'And for you, a newcomer to the district, the position must be a severe shock. You will need much courage during the next few weeks. Be patient and seize your opportunity as soon as the wave of fanaticism has passed.'

The vicar glanced over the tombstones at the withered yew tree by the gate. Its stark crooked boughs were outlined against a glow of lamplight from the bedroom and parlour windows of the Nances' home just opposite. This reminded him of Rosa, the flame of carnal beauty that had haunted Beale's pits but was now veiled and ambiguous, potentially as dangerous to him as Bert. Mr Reed sighed.

'If I am to help these people, I must learn to understand them,' he said. 'And I simply don't know where to begin.' He hesitated, drawn by the spell of Beale's mood away from the surface levels of the problem. As he floundered deeper his hands jerked agitatedly in blind fretful resistance. 'If — if this Rock you mentioned yesterday were an ancient Druidical stone I could understand such primitive folk reverting at times to the tribal rites of their ancestors. But it is clear from the general talk that there is nothing in the least Celtic or even pagan about the stone.'

'No, I'm afraid there isn't,' replied Beale grimly. 'The dupes themselves seem to identify it with primitive Christianity. This is an outbreak of something akin to the hysteria at Lourdes: that is what makes it so dangerous to our progressive church life.'

'Is anything known about the origin of the Rock?'

Beale shrugged. He was again completely masked and impassive.

'A good deal of mystery still surrounds its actual origin,' he said with brusque detachment. 'Parson Bully spent several years investigating the matter, trying to sift truth from legend, but in the end he had to abandon the attempt. All that is tolerably certain is that Potter brought the Rock across Priory Bridge — presumably at night — in fairly recent times: I'm sure it wasn't in his lane when I began living at the manor. Mr Bully was of the opinion that Potter stole the Rock from one of my clayworks, and that the powerful sense of guilt it seems to communicate is the result of his theft. But I made the fullest enquiries at all my pits on both sides of the river, and am satisfied that no such slab of stone was ever removed by stealth from any of them. I fear, therefore, that on this point Mr Bully was deceived. The Rock is indeed Potter's and its peculiar atmosphere is, I believe, due to certain sacrificial rites connected with the barbarous idea of expiation or even exorcism.'

A cold wind blew through the churchyard. Mr Reed shivered.

'The whole thing closes round one like a nightmare,' he remarked passing a hand wearily across his forehead. 'If Potter had really committed such atrocities it would be a great relief to me to hear that he had been brought to justice — or that he had died,' he added with a touch of bitterness.

'And a great relief to me, my friend. But I can offer no hope that we shall be rid of him in the near future.' Beale stretched out his arm and tapped the granite cross above the nearest grave; he looked gloomily upon the cross. 'You will have to contend with the same odds as Mr Bully, and I could ask no more of you than that you would emulate his courageous spirit. So successfully did he resist Potter that during the whole of Ashford's ministry there was not a single instance of anyone in Carn Veor going to Potter's Lane.'

'The fresh outbreak seems specially timed as a challenge to myself,' complained the vicar.

'Possibly it is. But if you accept the challenge as vigorously as Bully would have done there is no reason

why you should not win through as he did. You will be
encouraged and stimulated as you learn of the terrific
battle he waged before he was laid to rest within these
walls.'

Beale nodded his head, pointing across the cemetery
at a tall rounded headstone at the bend of the path
marking the grave of Mr Bully.

Mr Reed looked but said nothing, and a minute later
Beale had gripped his hand in farewell and hurried from
the churchyard. The vicar heard his footsteps quicken
with deliberation as he passed into the silent Square,
then grow faint and confused on the rough stones of an
alley near the Yellands' home.

Beale was heading into a lane which led past Carn
Veor claywork eastward to the river.

Chapter Eighteen

JOE and Bronwen were sitting, separated by the width of the hearth, in the lamplit kitchen of Bronwen's home. Warmth seemed to have been drained from the room, though the fire had kindled in the open stove, blazing with a brisk crackle of white clayey wood recovered from the sand-dump.

The unexpected rebuff which Joe had received on telling her his news had put both of them on guard, tense with the knowledge of change and betrayal. There had been no love-making between them: Bronwen knew that if she relaxed in a gesture of tenderness it would mean a more horrible exposure of the nullity which had fallen on their relationship. She would be really unaware, untouched: the spirit was gone from her. Even though they did not repulse each other, something would be withheld. The physical thrill would be deadened, as if Nature were exhausted by the mere fact of being untransmuted in the hour of crisis. Their bodies had become substances of matter that might be jerked into positions and contacts which should yield mutual pleasure, but would yield nothing but irritation, a sense of impotence, of a ban imposed from without, from the heart of the struggle between Beale and Potter. And they knew what had begun this paralysis — knew that Joe's acceptance of Beale's offer of work had swept them to the obscure verge, the fading out of the mere human relationship.

Joe had taken an old newspaper from under his cushion, and looked over it, without reading it, until tea-time. He glanced occasionally across at Bronwen, who sat on the bench. Always he found her staring at him, unwitting and submerged, her face pale, haggard above the blue pinafore.

She prepared tea at four o'clock, and they sat together at the table. They ate little and felt no delicious sense of privacy such as they had known in Joe's bedroom and in the Gools' kitchen sometimes when his parents were outdoors. Everything was as dry and tasteless as the food they nibbled at.

When they had finished the meal — having exchanged throughout only a few halting remarks about the weather and their food — the tension increased; and as dusk fell the gloom within them became a cruel oppression. Joe again took up the newspaper and Bronwen fetched some knitting from the front room. She lit the lamp and then sat flicking the needles while he read.

Joe waited, hour after hour, for some change, a development that would restore normal intercourse between them. He felt unable to return home until this strange crisis passed, leaving them alert and practical as before. But as his eyes fumbled along the headlines of the newspaper, many of them accounting Beale's activities in promoting the cultural advance of the county, he became increasingly entangled, fogged by the sense of the ubiquitous movements of this dark personality.

It was the chiming of the clock that at length roused him. He tossed the newspaper on to the floor and counted the strokes as they bristled upon the silence. Ten o'clock! The knowledge pricked through to a nerve of decision, drawing out broken images of the normal external world outside these rooms. He could not stay here much longer. Timothy would return soon, and his parents were no doubt anxiously awaiting the

191

verdict he would bring back, the news of Bronwen's reaction.

Joe shifted upon his chair, pulling it nearer to the bench, and blundered into a fretful query.

'What's matter, maid? We've had a pretty evening of it! Aren't 'ee pleased with this offer o' Beale's?'

Bronwen had been casting about within the darkness for the explanation of her recoil. She had been awaiting some such question, and her reply came fluently, with a firm deliberation as she dropped her knitting on the table.

'No, Joe, 'tis true — I don't like it. 'Tis queer how Beale hasn't spoken about it before; he must have known you've been needing work. I believe it got something to do with your going to Priory Bridge yesterday. Beale heard o' that and thought he'd make a move of his own. He wants to use you to hit back at Potter, that's all.'

Joe blinked at the lamp that was burning feebly.

'Beale can do that if he like,' he said, 'so long as we profit by it.'

'But we couldn't.'

'Bound to if I got the money.'

'No. Not in the long run . . . We're so weak, and they — Beale and Potter — they're so strong and deep in what they plan.' Her lips quivered; suddenly she writhed.

'Oh, Joe, why've we got to be dragged into this squabble at all? We're born to it here in Carn Veor. We can't do anything — love or get work — without Beale or Potter using it for their own ends.'

Joe stood erect, and leaning against the mantelpiece he glowered across at her.

'You want to hole me back, I can see that,' he said tensely.

'No — only from ruining both of us!'

'Ruin! 'Tis marriage I'm talking of. Seems you don't want us to be made man and wife.'

'We never could be if you took a job with Beale,' replied Bronwen, speaking with feverish conviction. 'Or if we could — what would it be if — if we still felt like we do now? Don't you see, Joe — they can stop us *feeling* anything, they wi' their eternal wrangling over our bodies and souls. And Beale — you know how he always gets to work when a chap's in thick with him.'

Joe's sharp face had reddened; he breathed quickly.

'I shouldn't see much o' Beale just by taking a job under'n,' he declared. 'What sort o' love do 'ee think mine is? I aren't no evil-liver, and Beale hisself couldn't make me one. 'Tisn't in me to treat a girl like the rough claywork fellows do.'

'There's no telling what you would be once you got in Beale's debt,' replied Bronwen, passing a hand wearily across her forehead. 'The money that kept us together would come from Beale, and he'd have a say in our affairs.'

'What nonsense! How could he —? He'd never darken our doors.' Joe set his chair within a yard of the bench, and sitting down he pointed at her accusingly.

''Tis these old tales o' Potter's Rock what've put you off. You'd have welcomed this chance if it hadn't been for they.'

'No, I shouldn't. You're blind today, Joe. You knew better yesterday. I've feared something like this ever since . . .'

'For goodness sake don't go raking up that fête business! You're always harking back to that. What's it got to do wi' this?'

''Tis the same hands — offering me something . . .'

193

'Well, what harm could it have done to let Beale put a few flowers on your head?'

'Ask they Sprys: they know what it did to Elsie.'

''Twasn't Beale who jilted her when she hanged herself.'

'But she didn't start running wild till he touched her. Everybody saw the change . . . Have you ever thought what might have happened to me if I'd let him crown me?'

Joe was drawn down with her, coarsened and entangled among the roots of this underworld.

'D'you think you'd have hanged yourself?' he flung out, glaring at her with a strange, impersonal brutality.

'I might — or started haunting the pits like Rosa. I've seemed light and playful in being true to you, but there's been fear under it — fear o' Beale and — of those other things — down in the *wrong* lane: the rats eating the dead horse, the well with blood in it . . .'

'That's all morbid — and right off the mark here. 'Tisn't rats and horses you're thinking of now — 'tis Potter's Rock.'

Bronwen nodded moodily.

'I know,' she admitted. 'I can't help it. It's made such a difference to Maggie and George. I saw them this morning. And look at Bert.'

'I don't want to hear anything about that,' said Joe impatiently. 'Here's me with a good opening from Beale right after Potter slammed the door in me face, and not a word agin it except what I get from you! If that's all you care . . .'

Bronwen tried desperately to emerge, to touch a normality from which she could warn Joe of danger.

'Now we're going to fall out!' she cried vexedly. ''Tis all through Beale. I wish to goodness you never met him! He's got a hold on you already, I believe, and

194

here's what 'tis doing — coming between us. This is the first tiff we ever had.'

'And whose fault is that? If only you had sense enough . . .'

'It isn't my fault. I'd given up hope of you coming here again.'

'And you're sorry I've come — sorry I've brought good news! Of all the contrary . . .' Joe's fists clenched, he wavered again to his feet.

'There isn't another maid in the village who'd let me down as you have!' he cried, his voice now reedy and shrill. 'If you really loved me you wouldn't care what conditions Beale laid down — even if we had to leave Carn Veor and live wherever he chose to set us up. There's girls who'd go to Helburn pit itself if they could be wi' their chaps. Why don't you feel like that about me?'

'Because I aren't *quite* mad — not yet, though this is nearly too much for me! Father in thick with Florrie — marrying into the *heart* of this evil — that would have been bad enough without — without you too throwing it in!'

'Mad! You're mad enough!' retorted Joe. 'Talking so wild about nothing at all. Look at it wi' your plain common sense . . .'

'We can't. We're being drawn into something bigger . . . There must be a break, Joe, for me if not for you. We can pull back even now. Only refuse Beale's offer . . .'

'As if I could! 'Tis that or nothing now. And if you don't want to benefit by it I — I'll find some other maid who do, that's all!'

She was roused, surprised by a sudden stinging derision of him, a contempt for him in the body. Her face had a strange grossness, her lips curled, ugly.

195

'You'd better try!' she taunted, her eyes flashing full into his. 'It won't be as easy as all that! D'you think you're a Bert Truscott? If any girl saw *you* stripped to the waist . . .' She laughed hysterically.

Beneath the torpor of incredulity Joe was maddened; he could have struck at the dissolved unknown face thrust up towards him. But he obeyed the more superficial instinct, the urge to flee from the unknown, out into the commonplace village world, to the girls who did not share Bronwen's crazy fear of Beale. He stumbled, red-faced and inarticulate, towards the door.

Bronwen watched him, the wave of hysteria subsiding into her former mood, the dazed, impotent sense of inability. She could make no further appeal or protest; the lacerating taunt was the limit at which her love recoiled upon her and disintegrated.

But before Joe had entered the passage there came a sharp knock at the door, the latch was lifted, and a rough feminine voice astonished them both by announcing:

''Tis only me!'

The impact of a prosaic voice from the outside world tended to break the uncanny spell that had fallen upon them. But the speaker was Mrs Yelland, and this gave the interruption a strange potency — as if the visitor were somehow more than a mere person entering upon their nightmare from the village. She too was distorted, but by another element — the will and movement of Potter.

Neither Joe nor Bronwen spoke as Mrs Yelland, hatless and wearing a white apron, came into the room. She looked piercingly at them both, aware of the tension but regarding it as something inevitable.

'So you got Joe here for the evening!' she observed in a casual tone of suppressed urgency. 'Your father

196

out to Beale's, I believe? A bad move — I've heard of it.'

Bronwen slowly roused, gaping resentfully at Mrs Yelland.

'What've you — dropped in about?' she faltered.

'Not about that — 'tis Ellen Pascoe . . . You know I've said ever since she went in Potter's Lane that there must be a secret in her life what kept her shut up. Well, I was a true prophet.'

Mrs Yelland paused, noting the listlessness and irritation with which her news was received.

'There's so much happening in Carn Veor folk don't know who to talk about most,' she continued. 'But poor old Ellen'll get as big a share as anybody now, I believe.'

'Why — what's she been up to?' asked Bronwen.

'It seems that just after William Grose died, Ellen went to the vicarage one evening on some church business,' Mrs Yelland replied. 'That was the time Parson Bully was working to throw out Potter's by-law about married couples having to go to the Rock. Bully was a bachelor and — well, I suppose the subject got him a bit over-excited.'

Bronwen shrugged.

'Oh, so it's that sort of thing again? Ellen and Parson Bully this time. Very pretty!'

'No, it didn't go as far as that,' said Mrs Yelland hastily. 'Ellen been around telling the neighbours this afternoon that Bully put his arm round her and kissed her. That's all 'twas — nothing very bad, or she'd have reported him. But seeing the Rock last Sunday brought it back to her and made her feel guilty. She minded what fire there was in Bully when he quashed Potter's law, and she felt he might ha' got some of his fire from they kisses. And now,' — Mrs Yelland raised a hand as she stepped forward — 'something more have happened. I had to come over and tell 'ee as soon as I heard it.'

'About Miss Pascoe?' Bronwen's voice was dull but more agreeable. She had begun to emerge.

'Yes. Potter been waiting for Ellen to confess that she'd kissed Bully,' answered Mrs Yelland. 'And when that had been cleared up he sent his servant this evening with orders that Miss Pascoe was to set out on a long journey. She couldn't have understood at first, but it meant love for her too. William Grose's name was the last word she spoke when Mrs Nance went in, hearing her call. Miss Pascoe died a hour ago.'

A cry escaped Bronwen, and for several minutes a tense silence gripped the room. Mrs Yelland watched the pair, briskly compassionate. She stepped nearer to Bronwen.

Joe scowled at her over his shoulder.

'What's that got to do with us?' he demanded angrily. 'You needn't come in here gabbing about corpses.'

'Your love will soon be a corpse,' retorted Mrs Yelland, 'if you don't do as Miss Pascoe did last Sunday.'

Bronwen looked into the fire, moodily and with agitation.

'I daresay you've noticed, and 'tis true,' she said. 'Me and Joe have falled out here, and don't know what's happening.'

Mrs Yelland laid a hand on Bronwen's shoulder, stretching the other towards Joe as he stood hunched by the partition.

''Tis Potter calling 'ee in all these upsets,' she declared. ''Tis just showing 'ee you aren't able to manage your own life or keep your own love alive. You know where to go now so many in Carn Veor have found what they wanted.'

Mrs Yelland took up Bronwen's half-knitted scarf and tossed it to the other end of the table.

'Go along now, both of 'ee,' she urged. 'You've had warnings enough this week-end — Joe going so blind down to Priory Bridge, as we all saw outside Budge's shop — and now here squabbling . . .'

Bronwen shuddered.

''Twas more than that. We've felt — a horror — as if Beale himself was here in the room.'

'I know. We got to feel that before we'm drove. 'Tis a close shave for 'ee, and unless Potter steps in soon I'll wage you two won't be married.'

'I'm sure we shan't,' confessed Bronwen. ''Twas that very point . . . Joe wants to let Beale help us, and I won't never abide that. I'd rather stay single, feeling what I did that day o' the fête . . . But he don't see — he can't think of anything except that he was served so bad yesterday . . .'

She rose, and stumbling past Mrs Yelland she caught Joe's arm imploringly, her eyes stricken, beseeching him.

'I'm willing,' she murmured. 'Potter was cruel . . . but it can't be as bad as this. The Rock — Joe, it *is* different! Say you'll go with me — *there*; we *must* have all we've dreamed of . . . I know I'm going to the lane — I can't help myself. And you must come too . . . Will you, Joe?' She kissed him.

Joe bent his head, stolid, uncomprehending, but subdued at last.

Chapter Nineteen

WHEN Beale left him the vicar gradually shook off the fantastic mood into which their talk had thrown him, and took note once more of his surroundings. He was standing beside a grave and he looked down upon it. In the moonlight he read the name on the tombstone and saw that this was the grave of the Rev. Ashford, his predecessor. A wreath of lilies had been laid on it during last week, but the warm sun had withered them, dried their sap, and left them as tufts of yellow rags clinging about the wiry, drained stems.

Mr Reed gazed fixedly at the grave, as if he expected some idea to be prompted by it, some suggestion that would enable him to draw the people of Carn Veor away from their foolish superstitions and listen obediently to him, their ordained pastor. He sought while his eyes probed the scabrous turf some means of turning the feet of these villagers into the paths of wisdom and virtue. No comforting sign was given him, only a small black beetle crawled from the grass and burrowed among the lilies.

Maggie Gumma in her distress had almost entered the churchyard last evening. But she had stopped at the gate; she had put her hand upon the spiked bar and then turned away from death towards life. Mr Reed, however, was inside the high wall, between the dead yew tree and the lightless church. Nature had failed him, and so had the altar without a dogma, the religion within mankind, the ideal. He was broken by his retreat from the revealed Absolute back into the geneal currents of human thought. This had begun the fatal process; he had learnt to adjust himself, and had inevitably reached the point where masked evil was received as an ally. And the ally seemed impotent even against the ranting of a boxer. It was cruel, mystifying.

The vicar straightened, glancing back at the dark windows of the church. From the house behind him on the other side of the road — the Nances' — a man's voice broke the stillness, growing louder, speaking with grave and jerky emphasis.

Mr Reed moved to the churchyard gate and listened. He could hear the words distinctly, and found that the speaker was the person who had just crossed his mind — Bert Truscott.

'Church was empty this morning, Rosa,' Bert was saying. 'I had all the flock at me open-air meeting. And why? Because they could see that something had *happened* to me. That's the point. They knew nothing hadn't happened to Parson Reed. He could only tell 'em they must try to keep the rules Parson Bully drew up after he climbed the tree outside Potter's Lane. And people's tired o' that sort o' talk. They can see it don't work. Bully and Ashford, what've 'em done to change us here at Carn Veor wi' all their schemes and committees? Think o' last year's church fête when the very devil was let loose here because Bron Cundy ran off to hide from Beale . . .'

Mr Reed scowled across at the house and raised his hand as if he would curse it. And immediately, as his nostrils twitched, he was surprised by an unmistakable smell of sulphur in the air. Peering sharply eastwards he saw that above Beale's oldest clay-pit a huge cloud of smoke had towered up. It was actually the signal of Beale's arrival at the pit, the beginning of his descent into the obscure reservoir of lawless power in which he would find temporary solace, releasing himself from the strain of the Carn Veor battle. Under this smoke-pall Florrie's nymphomaniac mother already lay naked on the pit-bed where her child had been conceived and born. Beale crouched above her. Nearby, in the glare of a floodlight, Florrie's father — also an inmate — was digging a grave. To the vicar, however, the smoke conveyed no hint that his ally had dropped the mask of benevolence. He watched while a great flurry of wind bore down from Potter's land upon the cloud and rolled it towards him.

Mr Reed shuddered, cowering in the corner of the gateway. And within his mind there flashed, strange and unbidden, some words he had occasionally read in his Essex Church: 'Come from the four winds, O breath, and breathe upon these slain, that they may live.' He knew that this referred to Bert and not to himself. Had Bert caused the dry bones to live? Were there even now, arising in Potter's Lane, those villagers who had responded to his challenge — arising re-clothed in that valley of vision . . .?

Rosa's voice broke in upon the confused images: and at once the wind ceased, the sky was clear as before; only a sense of nausea and weakness oppressed Mr Reed.

'It must be hard for decent, moral people to see that spiritual things are just as bad as — as the gross ones — here on Beale's land,' Rosa was saying. 'Harder for them than for us. I knew as a child in Potter's Lane that it was my *soul* that shrank from the thorn trees, shrivelled up like a dead thing; so I couldn't look to *that* to lead me to Potter. I looked to my body instead, that was my mistake. I couldn't bear for *all* my feelings to be crushed out. But they were last night.'

'Mine too,' said Bert. 'And when we're married . . . that'll be something new for both of us.'

'Yes. Oh, Bert, I am glad to think of it having a *home*
. . . Never again among the clayworks wi' the hard
sand and rocks, the wood and nails. I shan't have the
shadow of the engine-houses on me any more . . .'

The irritable depression deepened on Mr Reed as he
listened. His face, bent under the yew tree, looked
abject, hopeless. No such vision as Bert's or Rosa's was
for him; instead he felt now, in flesh and spirit alike, the
certainty of defeat. And thus brooding he heard no
further sound until, startling him, the door of the
Nances' home opened and Bert appeared.

Bert came down the path with a buoyant, springy
step. Not until he reached the roadway did he observe
the shadowy form beside the churchyard gate. He
paused, greeting the vicar in a tone that was at once
strained and impulsive.

'That you, Mr Reed? Did Miss Pascoe call on 'ee this
evening, sir?'

'I met her outside the vicarage on my way to church,'
answered Mr Reed, shrugging with distaste. 'She was
— er — mentally ill: I advised her to consult a doctor.'

Bert sobered, moving slowly across to the gate.

'That isn't what she needed,' he said quietly. 'She
just had to unburden herself like the rest of us who've
been to Potter's Lane.' He hesitated, scanning the
vicar's face for a moment. 'Me and Rosa now . . . Our
bad doings'll have to be put straight in a different way
from Ellen's. We'd like to have it fixed in Carn Veor
church — here in front of our own people — instead of
sneaking off to St Petroc registry office. We don't want
more courting: 'twould only make talk. We've decided
for the last Saturday in April, if you're willing.'

Mr Reed flushed, feeling an antagonism that went
beyond moral censure. He knew that Bert's influence
would be the chief obstacle to his recovery of spiritual

203

leadership in the village. His mind reacted in a flicker of spite; he stood erect under a bough of the yew tree.

'I regret,' he said stiffly, 'that under the circumstances, I should not feel myself justified in conducting such a ceremony.'

Bert did not seem much surprised, though his response was earnest and persuasive.

'You needn't doubt it's genuine, sir. We really made a new start last night — closer to you church folk.'

'I am sorry. I can only repeat what I've just told you; and the reasons for my decision should be fairly obvious.'

Bert went on his way down the hill into the village. He walked briskly, glancing back at Rosa's home as he turned the corner. The troubled frown had left his face: his happiness and its lawful fulfilment did not depend upon the good will of a vicar.

Mr Reed sighed as he stepped back into the churchyard. He glanced eastward at the tip-light of Carn Veor claywork, burning low down on the gravel cone, faintly illuminating the gaunt tip-structure. And like a wave that had been held in suppression there flowed back upon him the cruel lines he had read that morning:

> 'Where tip-beams like huge crosses break
>   The Cornish landscape into dim
>   Avowals that we martyred him . . .'

The voice of the soil was about him, the voice of the pagan soil was baying from every grave and every flower. And as he had fused himself with the corruptive earth that martyred Potter, so the power of the Rock was martyring him. He felt it assail him even in the echo of Bert's buoyant footsteps receding down the road, and in the sound of a chair being shifted in the Nances' parlour as Rosa, the strange baptized body of the harlot, new and awesome in its derision of him, passed into the back room.

He tried to console himself by thinking of Mr Bully, whose courageous stand for a scientific faith had temporarily checked the power of this barbaric Rock. But he found no encouragement in these reflections. Bully had been silenced for ten years, part of the dust of Carn Veor. Only the Rock remained in undiminished potency, moving and working from the overthrow of his denials, from the fact of resurrection beyond the rhythm of the soil, beyond the spiritual frontier, beyond the martyrdom.

Mr Reed stood, numbly isolated, his eyes groping for succour towards the light of Beale on the low dune of clay.

Chapter Twenty

JOE and Bronwen moved out of the silent village and along the road southward. The moorland was harsh, reduced to a shrivelled passivity in the hour of moon-rise. It stretched as a dried skin, wrinkled and scarred, between the gravel heaps and the grim buildings of clay-works. A few of these works were still active; the clank of waggons echoed from the pyramids, and at their tips, under the arc-lights, the refuse spilled out in little jets of white foam — tiny and derisive vomits that fanned out over the slopes, thinning into the lower darkness. In the sky the whitish clouds were also thinned, spilt into the darkness, being in relation to the moon what the clay-vomits were to the arc-lights.

Joe and Bronwen hastened blindly away from this raw landscape, harried by the knowledge that there was no strife or tension between these various features from which they could take comfort — no protest of the soil against the refuse, of the heavens against the clay. All was integrated, unified; they were a part of it all, in the stain of Beale.

Behind them on the hilltop the church tower stood, massive and watchful, settled congruously upon Beale's land, leaving the unity of mood unchallenged. Their backs were towards the church of the clay-lands as they faced Potter's Lane with the new knowledge, the quickening thrusts of the great disintegration severing the bonds of the spirit. They were not climbing from the murky depths of the clay to its sublime heights, but renouncing height and depth alike, the whole sphere of human possibility allowed them by the master of the manor.

The tip-light of Carn Veor works still burned, casting a pale glimmer along the encrusted slopes of the derelict, rain-broken dune. But this radiance vanished at the first curve of the dump southward to the road. The moon and the claywork light were both on the other side, and the road lay in the gloom of the cliff-face as Joe and Bronwen entered upon it. The day's sunshine and the keen frost that could now be felt in the air had hardened the spilled sand-packs, and the shallow parts were now firm and crisp to the tread. The pair stole quickly like dark ghosts over the blurred, uneven road. In the deeps of them, amid the plunging and breaking surfaces of their besieged nature, the memory of their walk here yesterday flickered as a remote signal. Joe stared into the vague whiteness above them, the ridged banks of the barricade. And dully he knew what he had been doing — heaping up the barrier against the coming invasion, the release of the avalanche from Potter's country. The visible symbol remained, looming uselessly as he had left it on sighting Bronwen and Mr Reed, oppressive and aloof now from his movements, the movements of a spirit in which all resistance had collapsed. He, the whole village and the manor had been overwhelmed.

Joe and Bronwen came blindly up to the rope that still barred the road to traffic. They bent beneath it with a shrinking of the flesh, as though they feared the lash of a scourge, and hurried beyond it into the moonlit calm and openness of the dale. They walked apart, silently, each absorbed in the personal pressure: Joe numbed under the fitful recollection of his journey along this road yesterday to Priory Bridge; Bronwen clouded by the association between this flight and her earlier attempt to escape from the hands of Beale. The association — and also the difference. For then she had fled to

207

protect herself, while now she had but one purpose — to be rid of herself through an act of faith, through obedience to Potter's law which meant death to her and the new life, the new bed for love, in the Rock.

She and Joe both glanced fearfully at the false lane, the refuge that led to the dead horse and the poisoned well, and passed on to Potter's Lane. Its interior, gloomily shrouded by thorn trees, was repellent as ever to their senses, but they were now in panic flight, muddying and trampling every nerve of their natural sensitiveness.

They stole between the hedges into a chill, fretful dusk. The trees greeted them with a blunted rasp of leaves. They stumbled on the uneven ground, keeping close together, breathing hard, jerkily. Bronwen's eyes were fixed always on the sky, which was more soothing than the queer mottled twilight lower down. Her face caught now and then a spilth of moon-shafts through the gripped rattling boughs. Its curves were less soft now, taut, harsh. Below her hat the thick gingery hair flounced gustily, blown sometimes across her eyes for a moment. Joe looked at nothing in particular; his gaze wandered, probing the ground, the hedges, the sky, Bronwen's face. It was to him a blank, dead face; his senses ached dully towards it, yet scarcely knew what it was. The features had become unsexed, somehow gone to the bottom, lying as silt, hidden and unfathomable. He knew that he was similarly faded, unreal to her. They were waiting to be rekindled by a flash from beyond, outside themselves. And they were sure that it could not come from the earth; it was not in the sap or soil, or any other revelation of beauty. It was the flash from beyond creation.

Not until they had passed several bends of the lane did either of them speak. Then Joe said:

'We shall know soon, maid, one way or t'other. We're in Potter's Lane and shall see what's here.'

'Yes — and I aren't afraid, Joe,' Bronwen replied. Her voice, like his, sounded strained, muffled. 'We must go on till we see the Rock: that's all I want to see now. What have changed Rosa and took fear from Maggie is what we need.'

She was still submerged; he could not feel or realize her. The loneliness and impotence came smotheringly, fuller and deeper upon him every moment.

''Tis a strange thing, though, for we clay country folk to touch,' he murmured. 'What it've done to Miss Pascoe proves 'tis a terrible power what can handle death as well as life. It do make me shrink. I feel all wrong with meself. I mind' — Joe swallowed painfully — 'how I nearly took Beale's offer and allowed it to part us, and the thought's plaguing me.' He glanced abjectly over his shoulder.

Bronwen could not free herself to console him. She too felt the weight of the incubus, the personal guilt becoming palpable, estranging. That they were separated from each other was as nothing compared with this sense of being separated from some ultimate goodness which, even in their most rapturous union, they would still have betrayed.

'They others was the same when they came in here first,' said Bronwen. 'Think what Bert and Rosa must have had on their conscience. If there was hope for them there surely is for us.'

Joe nodded; he could make no reply, but walked with head bent, the look of a condemned man on his face. Their footsteps thudded irregularly in the ruts of the lane. The wind grew more gusty, coming in sudden bruising darts along the hedge, spinning the bramble stems further down, so that Joe's and Bronwen's coats

209

were frequently hooked and torn on the barbs. But determinedly they pushed their way on.

Abruptly at one of the bends Bronwen halted and raised a hand.

'Hark! What was that?'

Clearly the sounds had come from the verge of a field a few hundred yards ahead — the shrill angry slap of the wind upon the hollows of a rock, and the flurried scraping of hard thorn boughs against a stone surface. Such noises were often heard on Beale's clayworks, but Joe and Bronwen knew that this was unique. The buffeting of the stone was part of the mysterious destiny that had swept them to the lane. It was the call from beyond, like an echo of the invading voice of Potter bringing storm to the soul.

Joe's cheeks had blanched, but his eyes glowed with the first flash of an awakening.

''Tis the Rock — we're nearly there,' he whispered. 'Are you — ready?'

'I think so. Anyhow we've got to face it. I couldn't go back now. I feel something would strike me dead in the lane if I turned to go back.'

Bronwen moved forward; she had almost to drag Joe along. The lane dipped steeply, growing darker and narrower until it was little more than a hedged path. The undergrowth became more dense, so that their feet padded silently over masses of trodden ferns and nettles; they often blundered into gorse and hazel bushes that obstructed the way. But even where they could not walk abreast they were always in physical contact, resolved that the first glimpse of the Rock should find them fused in submission.

And suddenly, as they followed the last curve of the track, they were smitten by the weird, unique, glare in the hollow. Moonlight glimmered across the marshes

210

that bordered the fields, jabbing through the screen of thorns as if in baffled search for the secret of the thing that was guarded, yet dominant there in the midst.

The Rock towered starkly above the trees — a broad, shapeless mass of white stone. Its base was embedded in the field, in soft soil, so that it leaned forward slightly, overhanging the lane and stunting some of the thorn trees, which had retaliated by scratching and clawing at its surface. Obviously it had been blasted. Its jagged edges were the result of swift, violent splintering: no tool had been used upon it. But the purpose of this blasting was obscure, marking a moment of descent into the conditions that beset the clay country. And now the Rock was utterly alien and removed. The impact was that of sheer miracle. Though it mediated knowledge it stood by itself in an entirely unknown dimension. It might have been a fragment of a meteorite, so foreign was its atmosphere to that of the clay-bed from which it had been wrenched. It was not a part of the earth or of the rational consciousness of man. There was nothing in Joe and Bronwen, either in their carnal or spiritual perception, that could have even faintly understood what it was or what it meant. The hollow was quite free from any sinister or ghostly influence — free also from any hint of pagan darkness and brutality. But as they crept into the shade of the Rock, a germ of apprehension began to form in them — an awareness that the bed they sought was accessible only through the mood that had caused Potter to blast the stone. They must share that mood or remain in nullity.

They halted before the Rock, still holding each other's hands; and inexorably the pressure of its strange disrupting power worked upon them. They had only to stand in subdued silence, gripped by the potency that reached them as they gazed past the thorns at the

211

scarred stone, the alien life of Potter that vibrated so overwhelmingly close to them. Gradually they were drawn into it, released from the burdening memories of their natural religion — memory of Priory Bridge fading from Joe, the horror of the rotting horse, the rats and the blood-stained well passing from Bronwen. As the memories flickered out there came a moment of oblivion in which they both sank to their knees. Bronwen was crying.

At length they returned to normal consciousness, rising blindly and groping to clasp one another. Neither spoke, but on a mutual urge they stepped clear of the shade of the Rock, advancing very slowly and quietly along the lane. They were soon beyond the hollow, climbing a slope where the granite hedges were low, without trees. The upper parts of their bodies were not in shadow here, and the heaving of Bronwen's breasts had a strange distinctness and potency against the glimmering marshes, as if they were heaving out of the silt of a dead world. Her arm was around Joe; they were wading up together through the gritty, dissolving beds of their former attachments. The spell of the Rock had in some way changed not only the personal essence but also the nature of the general moulding tide that enveloped them. The pressure of a dark wave, in which all their previous desires had been stained and cramped, was lifted, diverted, thrown back into remote distances. And as the new understanding of love flooded in they hurried forward, knowing that it would still be intact and adequate when they reached the familiar claylands.

Chapter Twenty-one

JOE and Bronwen emerged from the lane and slowly crossed the bare downland towards the village. No one else was on the road, and though on the clayworks the waggons were still slurring skyward and spitting out white gravel, this activity was no longer felt as a menace or an intrusion. They came presently in sight of the Gummas' home half-way across the level. Bronwen especially was relieved as they approached it, for the renewed contact with the normal, prosaic world, which would have broken the fragile texture of a dream-experience, had no effect upon the new medium of consciousness. It remained real, clarifying and absorbing the various sense impressions — the cosy house, the lamplight streaming through the kitchen and bedroom windows, and, as they drew abreast, the open doorway with the short, flabby figure of Mrs Prynne standing on the threshold.

Bronwen halted, dropping her arm, and smilingly greeted the old woman.

'Good-night, Mrs Prynne!'

The woman fully turned.

'Oh, good-night to 'ee!' And rubbing her blotched cheek she added:

'I'm sorry to hear about your father.'

Bronwen stiffened and again caught Joe's arm. But this reminder too was a little gritty thrust from the old life that could not really penetrate to disturb her.

213

'Beale may have a set-back there too yet,' she replied, rousing. 'And if dad does turn against me — well, I shall have Joe, and we'll be married all the sooner.'

Mrs Prynne nodded, fidgeting with a blue shawl thrown around her bowed shoulders.

'There've been queer moves here in Carn Veor lately, and no mistake,' she said.

'Yes. Joe and me have got the secret tonight that Mrs Yelland found. Don't know who 'twill be next.'

'You've been to Potter's Lane?'

'Just coming back. I'd felt the urge since Maggie spoke this morning, and we made up our minds when Mrs Yelland dropped in . . . Tell Maggie we've been, and that it's worked for us as for all the rest.'

Mrs Prynne lurched heavily down the path to the gate, hobbling because of her corns and speaking excitedly.

'There's news for Joe too, if that's where you've been.'

'For Joe?' Bronwen's eyes flashed, quickening towards him.

Mrs Prynne leaned over the gate, gripping its top bar, her shawl flapping in the wind.

'If you got anything to tell Maggie about Potter,' she remarked, ignoring Bronwen's query, 'you'll have to call with it when she d'git around again.'

'Why — is the confinement . . .?'

'Yes. Doctor was here a hour or two ago. And all going well, though the pains was bad for a time. She had a lot o' water around her: it might ha' been worse.'

Joe paid little heed to this news. His face, now completely in shadow, held a rapt, brooding look, the eyes turned towards the hedges that hid Potter's Lane. He was hardly aware of Bronwen's delighted exclamation:

'Oh, so it's over! I'd been wondering how 'twould go

214

off, and was a bit worried till I saw her this morning. Doctor'd said it ought to be a hospital job, so we knew it was serious.'

'Yes, he did say so, and I'm glad Maggie wouldn't give in to him,' observed Mrs Prynne. She tossed up her head contemptuously, her uncovered white hair fluttering above the shawl. 'I'd be ashamed to have a maid o' mine sneak off to hospital for her baby. Maggie had the guts to stick it in her own home, and I'm so proud of her as she and George is of the chiel. Lovely boy 'tis.'

'I can fancy how proud they are,' Bronwen's eyes smouldered, she clutched tighter at Joe's arm. 'But about Joe . . .?'

'You needn't be afraid. 'Tis good news there too — as good as Maggie's.'

Joe had roused and was watching her intently as she proceeded:

'Potter's servant came here tonight — called exactly as the baby was born. Funny how she knowed just when 'twould happen, but it seems nothing isn't hid from Potter, and she's bound to go where he sends her to. She called at Miss Pascoe's too, I believe — but 'twas a very different business there. You may have heard . . .'

'Yes, Mrs Yelland told us Ellen was dead,' responded Bronwen. 'A happy release for her. She's had a terrible lonely life: longing for Will Grose all these years, yet with nothing to look back on but a few kisses from Parson Bully.'

'Well, the servant stopped awhile after doctor went off — some kind she was. And then she spoke about you, and Mr Joe.'

'Me?' Joe and Bronwen both took a step forward, tense and expectant.

'That's it. Potter've lost one of his men who used to work a bit on the farm — Harry Rickard there next door

215

to 'ee, Bronwen. Chap's going back to Beale's clay-work: you know he was sacked from there after the fuss last year when he told his mates he'd been in Potter's Lane. But claywork do offer more money, and Beale's glad to take him back, I believe. And so Potter do want to give 'ee the chance, Joe; only he was waiting . . .'

'What for?' Joe asked the question very quietly; he was thinking of the Rock in Potter's field.

The woman's puffy face again relaxed, the bare gums grinning, pleasantly.

'Potter's a queer old stick,' she said. 'Got his own ideas and ways o' doing things. No good complaining about 'em at all. He told his servant to say that if you come through the lane tonight you'd pass here, and I was to ask 'ee to call down to Priory Bridge in the morning.'

Joe gulped, and gripping Bronwen's waist he turned towards the beacon, which loomed a hundred yards to the south-east, beside the village. Bronwen sensed his desire for privacy and stepped further from the gate.

'I felt — I felt something like this would happen,' muttered Joe. 'And the work — farm work, you say, the same as I tried for yesterday?'

'No. Potter had his little joke there too. Things is mixed funny in Potter's world. It seems his best farm — this side the river — is really a clay-pit — called Pentroth, or some such name.'

Joe was puzzled.

'But Harry Rickard's was real farm work — carting manure there above Tredoggett.'

'He hadn't seen the Rock, that's Potter's explanation so the servant told me,' answered Mrs Prynne. ' "All who see the Rock do get work afterwards in Pentroth Pit," she said; "there's no more dreaming in the fields for they. And Pentroth is bigger than any o' Beale's pits," she said — "even bigger than his oldest one where the fire is. And the clay from Pentroth is better than any from Beale's land. Only 'tis a secret pit," she said, "and casual folk who just want to shove along decent is never allowed to work there. But when Joe've been through the lane he'll be the right man," she said.' Mrs Prynne paused, clearing her throat.

'There's one clue I forgot, for 'tis rather mystifying. But this Pentroth work will include repairs on that old cave opposite the opening o' Potter's Lane. It got to be restored soon, for 'twill be needed, the servant said.'

'What for?' asked Joe.

'For all the folks who'll be going through Potter's Lane,' replied the old woman. 'I mind hearing that that cave was the real church o' Carn Veor — the place where the parsons used to get their power in olden times. And now Potter's expecting a big rush o' new followers and must have a house built for 'em to worship in. I was saying to Maggie this afternoon that we'll soon be needing a new church in Carn Veor if things go on at this rate. Parson Reed's won't be any good to they who've seen the Rock.'

Bronwen pondered: the spiritual horizon was broadening, revealing prospects she had overlooked.

'I hadn't thought of that side of it,' she admitted. 'But of course — we shall need to band together against Beale, and for worship, as you say, now we belong to Potter. And Joe's got to help to build the new church?'

'Yes. All the rubble got to be cleared away, and fresh walls built: for though Parson Bully made it a ruin the time has come to restore it,' said Mrs Prynne. 'There where Potter had his vengeance on Bully and pulled down Bully's tree, there you've got to raise a new house of worship — a house for reading Potter's book, for

217

prayer and breaking of bread. That was the servant's words.'

Bronwen was too deeply moved to remain longer talking with the old woman.

'Thank you, Mrs Prynne,' she murmured. ''Tis all wonderful news. 'I'll be in seeing Maggie in a day or two . . . Good-night!'

Mrs Prynne drawled her farewell and limped back into the cottage. Joe and Bronwen heard the door close as they moved over the flat road . . . Carn Veor was near: just one bend to turn, a bend shrouded by elms and blackthorns, and they would be in the familiar streets. They walked silently in the moonlight, unaware of it. There was a rhythm mingling of will in their movement, a new warmth kindling through the decayed mud-beds, forming a pasture of sustenance over which their desire flowed clean and free as a wind.

At length Bronwen spoke.

'Queer, Joe, isn't it?' she asked, probing his face as they halted a few yards from the corner. 'Everything's coming right all of a sudden. Only yesterday at Priory Bridge the servant said you wasn't fit for Potter's work.'

'I know,' replied Joe, eyeing moodily the clay-dump at the foot of which he had met Bronwen and Mr Reed; the memory of his labour on the barricade returned to him, he spoke in a subdued tone of conviction.

''Tis true what they've all been saying — they Gummas and Rosa and Mrs Yelland and Bert. There's no way o' getting favours from Potter except you go to the Rock; and when you've stood under it you know that all you've heard against him is lies. He's the friend of all we lovers when we go to him in the right way.'

Bronwen nodded.

'But why, Joe,' she asked '— why should Potter just put his Rock there in the lane and make a mystery of it

218

to attract folk instead of coming out in public like Beale
do and spreading the facts about himself? He'd be lots
more popular.'

''Tisn't for us to read Potter's mind,' answered Joe
gravely. 'He may have done things openly back in olden
times, before Bully's tree fell on the little church; and
maybe when the place is rebuilt he'll do things openly
again . . .'

Bronwen remained silent, her head bowed for a few
moments, then stepped on to a grassy bank that sloped
from the roadside up to the low field hedge. She reached
for Joe's hand and very quietly he followed her until
they stood together among the loose granite boulders of
the hedge-top, Bronwen supporting herself with a hand
against a small elm tree that sprouted from the bank.
They looked out over the village, down the scarp to the
illuminated pit-head workings of Carn Veor.

The scene was strangely remote to them, drained of
its menace. They were fused in the dawning recog-
nition, their fingers gripped hard, the surrendered spirit
seeking a flame that was no longer of the darkness. Here
as in Potter's Lane the old pagan creation seemed to be
in conflict with the new earth of their desire. Moon-
beams spilled upon them, broken by the elm branches
— pale and alien as the arc-lights that glimmered on the
blanched soil around the clay-pit and the gutted engine-
house. The carnal heart was burnt out, the new earth
triumphant.

Clemo: A Love Story
by Sally Magnusson

Against all the odds, Jack Clemo, the Cornish poet and writer, longed to be married. He had been deaf since his twenties and blind since his thirties, and lived in total dependence on his mother in a small granite cottage under the shadow of Cornwall's industrial claytips. And yet he still believed he had been made for marriage.

Then in 1967 a letter that was to change his life arrived out of the blue. It began, 'Dear Jack . . .' and it was signed quite simply 'Ruth'. Ruth Peaty, who was working in a Weymouth laundry, started writing to Jack Clemo because she was a compulsive letter writer, and because she shared his strong faith.

This book is the moving story of the letters, romance and marriage of Jack and Ruth Clemo. It is a story that many would have said was impossible.

Sally Magnusson is well known as a journalist, television presenter and author. She wrote *The Flying Scotsman*, the biography of *Chariots of Fire* runner Eric Liddell. She has also presented various BBC television programmes, including *Breakfast Time* and *Songs of Praise*.